Here the Dark

Here the Dark

A NOVELLA AND STORIES

David Bergen

BIBLIOASIS
WINDSOR, ONTARIO

FIRST EDITION

Library and Archives Canada Cataloguing in Publication

Title: Here the dark : a novella and stories / David Bergen.
Names: Bergen, David, 1957– author.
Identifiers: Canadiana (print) 2019023539X | Canadiana (ebook) 20190235403 |
    ISBN 9781771963213 (softcover) | ISBN 9781771963220 (ebook)
Classification: LCC PS8553.E665 H47 2020 | DDC C813/.54—dc23

Edited by Daniel Wells
Copy-edited by Allana Amlin
Text and cover designed by Ingrid Paulson

Published with the generous assistance of the Canada Council for the Arts, which last year invested $153 million to bring the arts to Canadians throughout the country, and the financial support of the Government of Canada. Biblioasis also acknowledges the support of the Ontario Arts Council (OAC), an agency of the Government of Ontario, which last year funded 1,709 individual artists and 1,078 organizations in 204 communities across Ontario, for a total of $52.1 million, and the contribution of the Government of Ontario through the Ontario Book Publishing Tax Credit and Ontario Creates.

The author acknowledges the support of the Canada Council for the Arts.

PRINTED AND BOUND IN CANADA

The following stories have been published in various magazines. *Never Too Late* and *Saved* in *The Walrus*. *April in Snow Lake* in *Prairie Fire*. *Leo Fell* in *Toronto Life*. *How Can* n *Men Share a Bottle of Vodka?* won the CBC Short Story Prize and was published in *Saturday Night*. *Hungry*, nominated for a Pushcart Prize, was published in *Hobart*.

April in Snow Lake

✻

1.

THE SUMMER I turned nineteen my girlfriend went to Italy to work as a cook for a crew that was rebuilding houses in the aftermath of the earthquake in Udine Province. She wrote me long letters on thin sheets of paper. The letters arrived two weeks after she wrote them and as I read her words I was aware that what I was reading had already passed, she had moved on to some new experience, and so I felt as if I was following her from some great distance, catching a brief glimpse of her, only to have her disappear into a future that I would hear about fourteen days later. She had met a wonderful group of people from Belgium and Holland and France. There was Paul, who was six-and-a-half-feet tall and played the banjo and admired Woody Guthrie. He wore a bandana. And there was Lillian, who was German Swiss, and was teaching her French. Lillian had taken her to Venice one Sunday, on their day off, and they had stayed overnight in a tiny villa. They had shared a bed and woken in the morning and made coffee on a hotplate and then had leaned out the window of their room and watched the lovers pass by below. It is all so romantic, she wrote. When I read this I was forlorn and I wondered how I would last the rest of the summer without her. I had found a job driving a truck for the local feed company, a job that required a lot of sitting and waiting, usually in the lot of an abattoir where I had been sent to pick up several tons of meat meal. Every evening I showered and scrubbed myself in order to remove the smell of dead animals from my hair and skin.

A year earlier I had decided to become a novelist, or a writer of short stories, or a poet, though I did not truly understand poetry and was more attached to narrative crescendo. I would write in a frenzy over the weekend and show my stories to my girlfriend on Monday evening. Of course we talked about my lack of life experience and my lack of voice and my lack of worldliness. She thought that my religious background, my faith in God, how I saw the world, would be a detriment to my writing. She said that Ernest Hemingway's father had been religious like my father was, but that Hemingway had managed quite nicely to walk away from all the baggage. I said that I had no desire to walk away. There was room for grace as well as sin in the world of novels.

One morning, before I left for work, my girlfriend telephoned from Italy. At first I didn't know it was her because I had not expected the call, and then when I finally recognized her voice I told her that I missed her horribly and I couldn't wait for her to come home. She said that she knew that but she planned to travel after finishing at the work camp. She might visit Lillian in Basel and then hitchhike up to Amsterdam where Paul lived. I'll be home at the end of the summer, she said. Then we'll get married.

This had been our plan, to marry in the fall. It had been my idea, my wish. She would just as happily have moved in together, but I had convinced her that we should marry. She agreed. But first, she said, she wanted to spend time travelling. She was quite willing for me to join her but the offer felt too easy. She knew that I could not afford it.

Her voice on the line faded in and out, and there was a delay, so that our conversation overlapped. At times we were speaking simultaneously and then we had to repeat ourselves and this led to long silences while we waited for the other to speak, and then it started all over again. Finally I just let her talk and as I did so I was aware of the tremendous physical distance between us and that her heart seemed smaller. And then the line went dead. I sat beside the phone for half an hour but she never called back.

That week a letter arrived in which she informed me that she wasn't sure anymore if we should get married, in fact she wasn't clear about her love for me. She claimed that the world was a big place and that she had one life and was she ready to spend that life with me? She wasn't sure. I knew, as I read the letter, that the words had been written before her phone call, and this fact made our conversation irrelevant. She had been talking to me on the phone, promising that she missed me, and that she would return in the autumn and we would marry, while all along she knew that this wasn't true. The space, the geographical distance, and the gap between what she wrote and what took place after she wrote it, all of this depressed me.

Why had she not told me the truth? What was she afraid of? Was there something about me that she feared?

2.

TWO WEEKS LATER I quit my job driving truck at the feed mill and I rode a bus five hundred miles north to Snow Lake where I worked construction for an old friend of my father who was pouring basements. The crew worked long hours, getting up at five in the morning and working till nine or ten in the evening. The summer nights were short and the light was forever blue and then white and then briefly yellow, and again blue. We did not sleep much and this did not seem to matter. Because darkness barely existed, it felt as if sleep was something that other people might require. Not us. Perhaps it was a madness to behave this way, and perhaps this is why the summer lacked a moral focus. The lack of sleep, the wild dreams when I finally did sleep, the anguished poetry I wrote to my girlfriend, my predilection for feverish musings, an inclination to save the world from sin—all of this might have been the result of some great forfeiture.

I was not a drinker, and at nights, when the men were finally free, they went to the local bar while I stayed in my motel room, or sat out on a chair on a rock and read John Steinbeck. And the Bible. The other men on the crew, mostly older than me, kept trying to drag me down to the bar for some intercourse. This was their way of talking to me. I told them that I was engaged to be married in the fall. Shit, they said, that's exactly why you need to get laid. I smiled and humoured them and shook my head. They went off to get drunk and find a woman, or at least to imagine that possibility, and I read.

They had taken to calling me Preacher, because I had let them know that I was a Christian. That fact amused them.

On Sundays, our day off, I was lonely and so I wandered through the town. I noticed that the children on the streets and in the yards were aimless and, my nature being inclined towards industry, I decided to organize a Sunday Day Camp for youth. The ages would be 14 to 17. I didn't want any small children. I planned to do some hiking and orienteering and I planned to tell these kids stories that were mature and I planned to save their souls. I knew that a sixteen-year-old was able to think along the lines of metaphor more easily. At the local hardware store I purchased several compasses, a filleting knife, a hatchet, and two fishing rods. I canvassed the town, knocked on doors, and asked if there were teenagers living there who might be interested in joining my Day Camp. We would meet under the shelter at the town park. Some folks said no and closed the door, others were willing to listen, and one older woman who had no children asked me in and brewed tea and we sat in her dark living room and listened to the clock tick on the mantle as she cautioned me against presumption.

The first Sunday, three kids appeared. Two sisters, Beverly and April, and a boy named Rodney. I told them a little about myself—I was nineteen, I came from a small town in the south, I liked to read, I wrote poetry and songs, and I believed in God. I asked them to tell about their lives. They looked at each other and giggled. Finally April said that she was there because her younger sister Beverly wanted to come. She shrugged. April had long dark hair that she wore in a single braid and, unlike the other two, she looked right at me when she spoke. She was seventeen. I found her very attractive and so I concentrated on Beverly and Rodney, sneaking looks at April when I thought she didn't notice.

That afternoon I taught them how to build a lean to, and how to use the compasses, and we caught two fish and filleted them by the lake. These were all things that my father, who considered himself a bit of an outdoorsman, had taught me. We built a fire using the log cabin method and we fried the fish and ate it with our hands, right from the frying pan. Later, I played a few songs and I sang and then I told them the story of how I had become a Christian. I had asked Jesus into my heart. Everyone needs to do that, I said. Would you like to do that? I asked. They looked at me and then April said, Maybe. Someday.

That's good, I said. Really good.

That night I went to bed imagining that I might fall in love with April, or if not that, we would walk in the park at the edge of town and hold hands. At that time in my life I was full of ego and pride and I could not imagine April liking anyone more than me, in fact I thought that if I were to be with her, I would be the gentlest and kindest person she had ever known. These were similar to the thoughts I used to have about my girlfriend.

I had not heard from her since the last letter, and though I had asked my parents to forward my mail, no letter had arrived. I believed at the time that she would come to regret her decision.

ON THURSDAY EVENING, three days before the next Sunday meeting, I was out walking when April rode past me on her bicycle. She was going in the opposite direction, on the other side of the road. She slowed down and stopped and straddled her bike. It was late, but it didn't feel late because the sun had just set and it would rise again in several hours. She was wearing jean shorts and a pink T-shirt and black running shoes. She had released her hair from the braid and it hung long and shiny. In the dusk, and from across the road, I could not see her eyes properly.

I see you walking, she said. Every night. Kinda stupid.

Why?

Nowhere to go 'cept in circles.

I don't mind, I said. The word stupid had surprised me. It sounded rough and wrong in her mouth. And forward, as if she were flirting.

She looked down the road back to town. You have a girl-friend? she asked.

I said I did but that our relationship was on hold.

What does that mean?

It means that we might get back together.

Is that why you go walking? You walk and you think about her?

She smiled when she said this, in a teasing manner, as if by talking in this way we were moving sideways into more open territory.

Beverly thinks you're cute, she said. Kinda like David Cassidy.

Ha.

And our grandma says to stay away from white boys.

To that I had no good response, and so I simply shrugged.

A half-ton approached in the distance, coming from town. It slowed and stopped. The driver, a man, rolled down the window and talked to April. The truck blocked my view of her and all I saw was the back of the man's head as he spoke. I couldn't hear anything. Then he put the truck in gear and carried on. The dust from the truck rose and settled and the night air grew quiet once again.

Uncle Frank, she said.

I waited. The gravel road between us seemed wider now, as if the half-ton, or the presence of her uncle in the half-ton, had created a rift.

And then I said something that I immediately regretted. It was not in my nature but it came off my tongue spontaneously.

I'm going to write a poem about you, I said. April in Snow Lake.

She was startled. Her hands went to her handlebars and she climbed back onto her bike. She looked at me with disdain, or so it seemed, and then she rode off. She did not look back. I raised my hand and started to call out, but I said nothing. My statement, I thought, had been a declaration of affection and admiration. I wanted to follow her and apologize, but she was already far away, riding quickly. A vehicle approached from behind me and I stepped off the road to let it pass. It was the same half-ton that had stopped earlier. The truck sped by, and in the distance I saw the lights of the rear brakes come on and the truck pulled to the side of the road. Dimly, in the failing light, I saw a man climb out, walk around, pick up April's bike and throw it into the bed of the half ton. April climbed into the passenger's side, and the truck disappeared.

THE FOLLOWING SUNDAY seven kids showed up. The original three plus four more. I was pleased with myself and imagined that the news had gotten around that I had something to offer. I had purchased some rope and wire from the hardware store and that day I showed them how to set rabbit snares. April seemed distant, though at one point she said that I had placed the wire too high, the rabbit would scoot right under, and she showed me her way of doing it. Her hands were nimble as she cut a branch and attached the snare. Her tongue touched the top of her teeth as she worked.

At the end of the day I asked her if she might want to walk with me one evening, maybe out to the shore of the lake. She smiled and shrugged and said that I could come get her. She lived in the yellow house on Larch. With her Uncle Frank. I managed to get off early Monday evening and, after showering, I walked through the town and found her house exactly where she said it would be. This surprised me and I wondered why it surprised me. Who did I think April was? She answered the door and stepped outside into the dusk and without a word we began to walk. Eventually she said that her uncle thought it was strange to go out walking with no purpose. What's the point?

You enjoy nature, look at the stars, smell the air. I said this with complete authenticity.

She sniffed the air but seemed unimpressed.

April was wearing a different coloured T-shirt, blue. Her bare arms were smooth and brown. I felt extremely lucky but I said nothing. We walked to the town park and sat on the swings and after a bit I pushed her and gave her an under duck, but where any other girl would have screamed and cried out, April said and did nothing. We sat on a bench and she told me a little of her history. She and her sister had lived with her mother in Winnipeg. She went to high school there for a while. And then her mother went away and her uncle, who worked in the zinc mine, took her and Beverly up north. There were four of them in the house, including her grandma.

The next night, Tuesday, we held hands at the edge of the lake.

Wednesday we kissed briefly. One time.

Thursday she asked if I was still writing *that* poem. And she laughed. She said, My uncle wants to go hunting with you. He heard you liked to snare rabbits and that you fish and stuff. He said he can learn something.

Friday, when I knocked at the door, her Uncle Frank opened it and said, Tomorrow we'll go hunting. He didn't ask if I wanted to go.

What'll we hunt? I asked.

Stope rats, he said. I'll pick you up at seven.

I WAS READY and waiting at seven the following morning. Frank showed up at nine wearing a checked jacket and jeans and heavy boots and a baseball cap that said Black Cat. In my backpack I was carrying my filleting knife, hatchet, a sandwich, an apple, and some rope. The compass was in my pocket. First thing he did was take my pack and look through it. Then he tossed it on the porch and said, Don't need that shit. Trust yourself.

I thought we might be driving somewhere but we weren't, we were walking. We walked out of town and cut off into the bush. He was a heavy man with short legs but even so I couldn't keep up with him. He walked straight into the bush and kept walking. The terrain was rocky, interspersed with swamps that he sometimes skirted and sometimes waded through. By noon my runners were soaked. At some point he chose a flat rock to sit down on and indicated that I should join him. He pulled a chocolate bar from his pocket and gave me half. He had a rifle, what he called his Winchester three aught eight, and when I asked him again what we were hunting he said, Animals. While we were sitting in the sunlight, not talking, a deer stepped delicately in front of us, about a hundred feet up the path, and lifted her head. I pointed. Frank had already seen her but he made no move to raise his rifle. The deer saw us, and bounded away.

Too far to drag out all that meat, he said. He stood, hefted the rifle, and carried on.

We passed by a waterfall at which we kneeled and drank from deeply. The sun was high and hot and I dunked my head and wet my arms and thought at that moment that the world I was in was beautiful and strange and that there was nothing to be afraid of.

Frank sat and lit a cigarette. Offered me one and I shook my head. He talked then. He said, If you get lost in the bush don't run around in fucking circles. It'll just tire you out. What'll kill you is the exposure and lack of water and your own panic. You think you're pretty smart, he said. He wasn't being mean, at least his face wasn't mean, but his words sounded dark and threatening.

I don't think that.

You like my niece. April.

She's nice.

'Course she's nice. Hell. You probably want to marry her.

Oh, I don't think so.

Not good enough for you? he asked, and he laughed. His laugh was high and loud and I realized that he wasn't laughing at me but at his own joke. He said, You have to pass a test if you want to be in the Greyeyes family. Two choices. Suck my dick, or catch an eagle with your bare hands. He laughed again. Slapped me on the back. He said, April knows the bush. How to snare and skin a rabbit, how to read the stars, the sun, the moon. She can shoot and gut and bleed a deer, quarter her, and travois her out of the bush single-handed. Bet she never told you any of that.

She didn't, I said.

She wouldn't. She's not a show-off.

I know that.

I hear you believe in God.

I do.

All them gods, he said.

He spoke quietly and with little inflection. He seemed to be talking to himself. I felt small and helpless.

We slept beneath a scraggly jack pine, on the soft bed of dry brown needles. We had no blankets. The mosquitoes were the worst at dusk. Frank built a smudge using the fire we had made earlier to roast the rabbit he had shot. I was hungry and ate the meager meat and then sucked the bones dry. Best meal I ever had. As we ate Frank talked. He said that when he was young, 'bout fourteen, he went to school in Alberta. Near Brooks. The kids didn't like me for some reason, he said. Beat me up every day. And so it was my stepfather who one day packed my satchel full of rocks and sent me off. This time when Roger Steingaart pulled my ears, I swung my satchel and spun and caught him across the temple. Knocked him out. That was that. No more beatings.

He stopped talking.

Did you get in trouble? I asked.

He chuckled. Funny, he said. That became my name. Trouble. Here comes Trouble. Look out for Trouble. But as you know, no one wants to tangle with Trouble.

That night, I tried to stay awake, believing that Frank would kill me in my sleep. Or that he would leave me to die in the bush. He'd seen me playing with my compass earlier. He asked to see it and then slipped it into his own pocket. Shit, he said, follow the moss on the trees. It always grows on the north side. I slept finally and woke at one point and he was still sitting by the fire smoking. I watched him for a long time and then I fell asleep again.

In the morning, he was gone.

3.

I MARRIED MY girlfriend, the one that went to Udine, a year after she returned from Europe. We are still together and she continues to read early drafts of my stories, offering advice, confirming at some point that I have moved beyond sentimentality into clarity. The first time I told her about April and Frank she said that the story was twisted, all upside down, and that's why she liked Frank. She said that the climax of the story was when I woke up and found myself alone in the bush. Right there, she said, that's a good moment.

I could have died out there, I said.

Not at all, she said. Frank knew what he was doing.

WHEN I FIRST realized that Frank was missing, I imagined he had gone into the bush to pee, or that he was out hunting and would return with a small animal slung over his shoulder. I sat by the dead fire for a time. Then I stood and walked out into the bush and called out Frank's name. My voice got lost in the trees and the land and branches and scrubby bushes. Not even an echo. Two hours later I realized that I was alone. I had a vague sense of the direction we had gone the day before, northeast, and so I began to walk so that the sun, when it appeared through the clouds, was hitting the left side of my face. For the first while I was dogged and focused and I kept track of the sun and, as Frank suggested, I kept checking the moss on the trees. And then, about noon, it began to rain and the sun disappeared completely and the trees all bled together and the rocks looked the same. And I ran. For a long time I crashed through the trees and the bushes, scraping my face and arms, falling and picking myself up, charging onward, until I fell. I stayed where I fell and I wept into the ground.

Eventually the rain stopped and the sun came out. Water dripped from the leaves and the branches of the trees. It was a calming sound. I stood and began to walk once more. I slept that night on a high rock beneath a small conifer. I pulled loose branches over my torso and legs and pulled my shirt over my head to ward off the mosquitoes. I was hungry. I was wet. I was cold. I had no way to make a fire. And so I prayed. I asked God to save me, to help me find my way out. I told Him that if He would do so I would serve Him the rest of my life. I fell into a busy sleep only to wake and imagine wild animals hunting me down. I sat up and hugged my knees to my chest and fell asleep in that manner. At dawn, when the shadows were dissipating, I resumed walking. At midday I came upon the waterfall where, two days earlier, I had washed my arms and dunked my head. I dropped to my knees and drank from the stream, raising my head finally to survey my surroundings, aware that I might find my way home. According to my calculations, this stream was three hours from the road.

Six hours later, exhausted and prepared to lie down and accept my fate, I came upon a logging road that eventually led to the highway where a man in a mining truck picked me up. He rolled down the passenger window and waved me over. He looked at me and said, God look at you.

I SAW APRIL one more time. I had to face her and I had to face Frank, and so I knocked on the door one evening and Frank answered. He didn't seem at all surprised. He said, Whoaa, where's the eagle? Or have you come for this? And he grabbed his crotch. Then he laughed his big laugh and slapped me on the shoulder and he held my chin with a rough hand and he went, Ahhh.

He went back inside and I could see April at the kitchen table, spreading peanut butter on a piece of white bread.

She looked up and grinned. I didn't know if she was smiling at her uncle's tasteless joke, or happy to see me. I couldn't tell. I never could tell with her.

Did you know he was going to leave me out there? I asked. I was still standing in the doorway.

She shrugged.

You could have warned me.

You wouldn't have listened, she said. She turned back to her sandwich.

The thing is, I could have gone in and she would have been fine with that. But she seemed to be fine with me not joining her as well. At that time in my life, at that moment, I could make no sense of how to choose. And so I stepped away from the door and I walked back to my motel room. Two weeks later I left Snow Lake.

DURING MY SECOND night in the bush—when I was still unsure if I would survive, when the mosquitoes attacked with ferocity and then just as quickly went away, when the noises of the forest fell down around me—I had a vision. I was a small animal. A vole or a chipmunk or some such little beast. I was alone. I was being hunted. I was running through the underbrush, zigzagging here and there when I came to a hole into which I tumbled. Inside the hole was a vast open space, and against the walls of this space, on chairs, sat a group of animals—beaver, muskrat, fox, bear, deer. They were drinking tea. It reminded me of prayer meetings I had attended as a young boy. Except here, no one spoke. I took a chair. The silence was disconcerting.

Where am I? I asked.

Silence.

Can you help me? I said.

What's the problem? the bear said.

I'm lost, I said.

Good to know, said the bear.

How Can *n* Men
Share a Bottle of Vodka?

❊

WHEN THE QUESTION was pierced, then plucked
from the dartboard and folded open and read,
Maxine Duras, with her feverish eyes, rusty hair,
small forehead and freckled arms, wanted to know why it was
just men and didn't women drink vodka as well? Her red hair
moved up and down with her shoulders. Her boyfriend, Rodney Alder, who had thrown the dart to perforate that day's
question, was still standing. I asked him what he thought. He
said it was a problem and he lifted his chin, offering his thin
neck, a rope holding the globe of his head, and I imagined
him in bed with Maxine, the sheer weightlessness of him
above the substantial organized fury of Ms. Duras. Sometimes I was astounded and awed that these children were
sexual beings. I could not imagine it: adolescents were too

happy, too exquisite, to be fumbling around with something imperfect. I shook off the image and said, "Sit, sit, Rodney," and so he sat, casting his eyes towards the freckled forehead of his lover, who loped her long hands through the air and, pre-empting Jimmy Skrivens, said that the question was more a matter of argument than any clever calculation and if n equalled twenty then there should also be twenty glasses and a fair pouring out of the vodka into those glasses until all the n were happy and could throw back the vodka. "Am I right?" she asked, and I had to admit that yes she was right, if ever there was a right because, don't be fooled children, I said, the idea of right and wrong was dreamed up by moralists and witch hunters and prudes and tee-totallers.

I threw my arms in the air and said "Enough, enough," and read off their assignment and left them stewing, the air suddenly solemn and filled with sharp little pencil scratches and the rub rub rub of erasers. I stepped across the hall to gaze through the tiny window at Jennifer Donne's English class, all in a circle, Jennifer's arms a thing of beauty, her head thrown back suddenly, wide mouth open in a roar of delight that came to me as from a silent movie, the door being closed. It was Jennifer who had suggested the dartboard with a series of problems pinned to it which was, she admitted, a bit of a trick, but then teaching was all smoke and mirrors, wasn't it, she asked, and ducked her chin. We were eating lunch that day in her room where the window looked out onto the football field and the figures of the soccer team at practice appeared as if through the wrong end of a telescope. I was eating crackers and drinking vodka from my sleek-looking Thermos of shiny aluminum when I told her that my wife had left me six months earlier for a Korean man with a small dick and her response was not one of solace or pity but curiosity, for she asked, "How do you know his dick was small?" I replied that I could not verify this but the statement was based on stereotype and in my shame and anger I was willing to abuse this notion. Saying this I fell into a tale of recent history, remembering the day I returned home from work to find my father, who was a near-invalid and lived with my wife, daughter and myself, standing, bags packed by the doorway waiting for a taxi. Seeing me, he began to shout that some man was upstairs having his way with Holly, my wife, and this was something he would never have allowed, never, and as the spume fell from his mouth I guided him back to his bedroom where he went to sleep. I ascended finally to the top floor of our big brick house where I found Holly lounging, fully clothed, in one of the rooms facing the street, the light falling through the window. It was a grey spring light, almost gone. Holly was alone. She had just showered and her hair was wet, her feet bare and she wore jeans and a black sweater and was working at her left foot with a nail file. I loved her feet, the ridges and lines and tendons, the definition, the length of her toes, the curve of her arch when pressed within a high-heeled shoe. I could see the outline of her hamstring through her jeans and the sight of this, the frailty it evoked, the sudden knowledge that we are made of blood and shit and neurons and cells that lead, through chaos, to the wonder of her hamstring, almost made me weep with grief and joy. She looked at me and her mouth flickered and the dull light through the dirty window made her eyes darker though I could still see the truth there and I bowed my head like a repentant child and said that I was stupid. She said that I wanted to be stupid, this was not the first, and then she began to cry and then more tears arrived and she said, "See, see," and I kneeled and held her till the light was sucked from the room.

Why I related this all to Jennifer Donne was not a surprise. I needed a gentle breast to fall upon and Jennifer was both gentle and ample, for she was a large woman, fat some might say, though I would not describe her so, perhaps because I found her attractive, and later, after we became lovers, I discovered that desire will always surprise us. That day, after my confession, Jennifer took my hand and she said my talents were prodigious, I had created a sense of place, had an eye for detail, and the telling of it was lyrical and poetic and she had, she said, fallen for the voice of the teller. I went home and told my daughter Natalie, who was thirteen at the time and had in recent months taken up witchcraft, that a colleague of mine had invited us for supper and she was divorced and had black frizzy hair and five children and there was something wild and woolly about her. Natalie said that five kids was scary and I didn't want to be leaping into anything on the rebound and she wanted no part in a blended family, no thanks, and I better watch out that this woman didn't style her way right into my bank account. She waved her hand at me through the haze of incense, dismissing me, so I went downstairs to find my father asleep and drooling in front of the TV. I woke him and walked him to the bathroom and pulled down his pants and he sat and looked at me and said he couldn't poop. "You can poop in the morning," I said, and I crouched beside his sour-smelling legs and raised his trousers. I took him to his bed where he put on his pajamas, sighed, and said that he should die already. "No, Dad, no," I said, and I left his light on, the door open. Then I went into the kitchen and poured myself a gin and tonic, a lime for pleasure, an ice cube, and I sat down in the darkening room and looked out at the street. A car passed, a boy on a bicycle, and I thought of Holly, my actor wife, and wondered where she was tonight. For several months now there had been no contact and Natalie was suffering that. I imagined a myriad of men lined up, wanting to share my wife: a breast, a leg, belly button, her heart-shaped ass, her mouth, her cunt, which I had loved to stroke, telling her she was beautiful, my shoulders pressed to her inner thighs, her insteps on my hips and her soft voice whimpering far above me. I still missed her, even though in the last year I knew I was sharing her, that I had become simply a number in a series repeating to infinity, a procession which included a blue-haired clown with large biceps; a Falstaff who had been flown over from England because no credible actor could be found locally; a bearded queen who was the son of a provincial politician and who acted fey parts and probably tried Holly's beautiful heart shape, though she made no mention of it and certainly would have if she had liked it; and sundry others, jack rabbits all, having Holly beneath my roof; and then finally, the tiny dictator, who had her the same day I found her barefoot on the couch and ached for her but could only hold her as she wept and asked me to see.

THE NEXT DAY I put the following on the blackboard, $(x + y)^2 = x^2 + 2xy + y^2$, and I said that Leonhard Euler once wrote this equation to prove the existence of God and that as a boy Bertrand Russell was forced to chant *the square of a sum is equal to the sum of the squares increased by twice their product* and though Mr. Russell did not know what this meant he feared the tutor would throw things if he got it wrong. Maxine

Duras said she understood, hmm, hmm, and Rodney Alder said he liked the allusion to God but wondered how the formula proved anything. I admitted that I didn't know, though I did know that once upon a time people believed in magic and then they believed in God and that today we believed in science and I was all for that because where would we be without science and logic and reason. I told Rodney Alder that because I was better at logic I could win any argument and I said, "Ask me a question, pose a problem. Anyone?" The class retreated, heads bowed, except for a few brave souls who smiled weakly. Then James Gerbrandt cleared his throat, lifted his sharp chin and asked, "How can n math teachers share a Thermos of vodka?" He looked around triumphantly, perhaps expecting a raucous backing. I hesitated and looked out across the empty air suspended above those thirty-one empty heads. A few titters rose and fell. I pondered my options and then I opened my Thermos, filled my coffee mug and said, "Water, with a hint of lime." I took a sip and asked if Mr. Gerbrandt should choose a dart and the class, like a sleeping elephant, roused itself and trumpeted, "Dart, dart." I waved my hand, brought forth silence, and said we would forgo the dart for a lecture. I said that the question was insolent, a betrayal of trust, and the point was that I had a personal life and was not a mere jack-in-the-box animated at 9 a.m. for their benefit and that yes children I did go home after school to a place where I ate, shat, wept and laughed and okay, I drank, but that wasn't so bad was it, and who of their parents didn't snooker a glass of something now and then and I said that the world was a cruel place and if there was anything at all to take the edge off the cruelty, find it and use it. The class was quiet and embarrassed and then Chrissy Tremblay raised her hand and said that I was not a bad person and that she liked me and that this was the best math class she'd ever taken. Other voices called out, "Hear, hear," and, "Me too," and, "Hey," and, "Yes."

Still, I suspected that James Gerbrandt was on to something, simply because I had acquired a taste and with that taste came lethargy and cynicism. I had stopped taking attendance in my classes only to discover that the students still came. I halted all giving of tests and found that no one suffered and I, certainly, had less marking. I introduced the dartboard and more and more of our classes descended into discussions on argument, logic and philosophy. One day we debated the merits of hallucinogens and three-way sex, which related in some way, one could argue, to an isosceles triangle, two sides being equal. Another time Brook Rice, a shy, articulate girl, used Liebniz to explain why things are so and not otherwise. That same day Jimmy Skrivens approached me after class and wiggled his long fingers as he talked about a poem he was writing which was, Mr. B., he said, related to Pythagoras's idea of number as the source of all things. I told him to read me the poem and he did. It was dream-like and made no sense to me and so I said, "Lovely words, lovely words." I immediately regretted the comment and shooed the poor boy off with a pat on the back. I found that I was resorting to irony and sarcasm. Cynicism had descended: not for the students but for myself, for what I was doing. I could not find my way through and imagined everything as rotten and wrong and I began to see the children I taught as rats conditioned to respond to buzzers, inane lines in thick textbooks, stupid questions, lots of stupid questions. And so, one morning I intoned, "Why, why, why?" and of course Maxine raised her hand and asked, "Why?" I bellowed at all sixty-two ears that if they believed that x equalled seven or thirty-six or nineteen, then they were wrong because x was crap just as n was crap, that was all, and I had spent my life searching for n, imagine that, and now I was leaving it to them, and I walked out the door and took the end stairs to the staffroom where I sat and drank coffee laced with rum.

JENNIFER TOLD ME that I was raging against Holly, my wife, and that instead of snapping at the students I should go home and hit pillows or go out hunting bear. It was noon hour and we were in her classroom and I'd just asked her for some poetry because my father liked to be read to in the evenings. Jennifer was standing by the window and then she turned with the poetry book in her hand and we both leaned forward and kissed. It was a rather longish and hesitant kiss, as if we were walking into an unknown lake. I put my arms around her and thought of a Butterball turkey. She was tight. I'd expected a laxness, flab, like approaching a waterbed, but her body was hard, even her big breasts had a trampoline quality. She smelled good and her mouth was a marvel. I explored it awhile and she made little noises, as if she were saying something and I thought how Holly, when we kissed, would be silent and concentrate on my gums, my tongue, the shape of my teeth. When we separated I looked at Jennifer and saw that a voyage out was not a simple matter and I went home that evening and again asked Natalie if she liked Jennifer Donne. She told me to settle down and so I asked my father the same question and in a moment of clarity he said that her loins were certainly fruitful.

The following week, around midnight, Jennifer phoned and asked me to come over and so I went and found her in her kitchen baking cookies and drinking wine. She told me to sit and asked if we could lap dance and when I said yes she showed me her breasts and pushed my mouth against her and then she had me stand and unbuckled me and pulled down my pants and sat me down and then slid one leg out of her jeans and panties and straddled me again clothes flapping at one ankle and she put me inside and said, "Oh." Dishwasher going, cookies baking, bright lights, her humming in my ear, the slap of her bum against my bare legs and then the quick gasps as she cried out that the baby was calling, hurry now, hmm, and then I was finished and she was off me and into her jeans and out the kitchen and upstairs to calm the baby. I looked around and pulled up my pants and waited. I drank a glass of wine and then another. Jennifer reappeared and sat across from me and said she hoped I didn't feel attacked. I shook my head and looked at her and considered that she was fine, really, with her bullish neck and small fingers and all those children like so many limbs and I pictured myself as just one more limb. Life with her would be matter-of-fact, simple and quick: the children would come first. Which was why we began to meet at noon hours, taking my Topaz out to an empty parking lot near the airport where we would fumble past our clothes to the bright edges of skin, shivering with anticipation, our foreheads knocking together, and I'd swim around her and she'd hoot and call out within our hard cave. She didn't ask, like another woman might, if she was too fat. Instead, in a highly erotic mix of math and sex, she said, "If you want to know my circumference, use your cock to find my radius."

HOLLY CALLED ONE evening, midweek, and at first I didn't recognize her. She was drunk, that was a sure thing. She said that the Korean actor had left her and she was wondering if I would have her again. My heart was doing strange things and my mouth was working up to a howl. To stem this I told her I had a girlfriend and that she had moved in with me and she had five children and there was no more room in the house. Holly asked how Natalie was handling that and then not waiting for an answer she said she wished we had had more children. I didn't respond. I could hear her breathing and I thought that if she were to come back, just show up at the door, I'd fold her in my arms and take her in and pull off her shoes and socks and kiss her bare feet. Then she said she needed money and I said okay and asked for her address. She gave it to me and later, after she'd hung up, I stared at it and thought that I could have gotten into my Topaz and driven over there. It was an apartment in the north end, close to the casino. But I didn't go, instead I poured a drink and called up Jennifer and said I'd had a dream and in the dream she and the kids were living with me in my brick house and that we were a big happy family and that she and I shared a bed and the kids had their own rooms and my dad ruled the main floor in all his naked glory and Natalie had given up being a witch. Jennifer said that I couldn't tell a thirteen-year-old what to believe and besides every girl that age did the witch thing and one thing for sure, before she moved in with me, I'd have to stop drinking. I looked at the glass in my hand and laid it gently on the windowsill and said that I could do that, no problem. After I hung up I looked at the glass and I thought about Natalie sleeping upstairs and how I should talk to her more and go to her volleyball games and be a better father. I thought about Holly and why she left me and I knew I could take some blame considering my love for the bottle, which she shared but not with the same devotion. Sometimes, when she was still with me, we would lie in bed happily drunk and the haze of alcohol made her float away from me and when she wanted to touch I said, "No, let's just look." My head and my heart were separate.

So, after classes the next day I unloaded my liquor cabinet and emptied the bottles into the sink. I took the beer cans from the fridge and dumped them. I cleaned out the cooking wine. When I was done I looked around the kitchen and thought that I should fix it up. I went down to the basement and found a can of yellow paint, a roller, and a brush. I had just started painting when my father walked in, sat down, and said that I should marry Jennifer. I asked him what he was talking about and he tilted his grey head and said that Jennifer was worth a thousand Hollys and that Natalie liked Jennifer and that it was time to supply some stability in my daughter's life and maybe once I did that she would stop dancing around a cauldron. I said that I had stopped drinking and that I had big plans to maybe quit teaching and find a different job, one that didn't suck the soul out of me.

I thought hard about what my father said, about Natalie and Jennifer and Holly, and at lunch one day, instead of having car sex by the airport, Jennifer and I drove to The Bay and looked at beds. We found this salesgirl whose name tag said Candace. She was wearing a tight black skirt, was skinny and tall, and she looked Jennifer up and down and her face went *whoaa*. I put my arm around Jennifer and said that we were newlyweds and were looking for a bed for the romper room. I winked at Candace and she led us over to a king size. Jennifer promptly sat down and rolled on to her back, legs in the air, wondering out loud if she would sink. "Come," she said, and she patted the mattress. I shrugged and laid myself out like I was preparing to die. "Relax," Jennifer said. She was wearing a low-cut blouse and a gold heart and a lot of perfume and I realized that this was the first time we'd been in bed together. It made me want to jump on her right there except anorexic Candace was hovering and still talking about size and strength. She asked if we wanted twin beds. Jennifer lifted her head and shook it so that her earrings dangled and spun. "Give us some time to think about it," she said, and waved a hand, dismissing her. Then she pinned me and I could see down her top to her lacy bra and the gold heart in her cleavage and she bit my neck and said that all five of her children had agreed, they could live in the big brick house and they were pretty excited, so how about that.

And then on Monday evening Holly called again and I said, "Don't call, I'm trying to stop drinking and talking to you won't help." She said that was good, really good, and then she asked how the family was. I told her we were fine, in fact we were just sitting down to roast beef and mashed potatoes and corn on the cob and spinach salad with roasted pecans and a dessert of apple cobbler. We were happy, I said. This took her breath away, I could tell, because the receiver creaked in her hand and she didn't speak and I imagined her mouth and the shape of her perfect little nose and then she said that I was lucky and that she wanted to be lucky too and then she hung up. I went back into the kitchen and sat down with my dad, who was in boxers and a muscle shirt, and Natalie, who was eating crackers and peanut butter.

The next day I told my math class that I was marrying Jennifer Donne. The girls in the class thought this was neat and they shook their heads and smiled. But the boys were

confused and it was James Gerbrandt who, indolent and pre-
dictable, asked, Why? I paused. Looked askance at James. The
other boys. Then I said that there were many reasons I could
cite: like how she so trippingly quoted poetry; or her multiple
offspring, five beautiful sprites; her gusto for lemon pie; her
Willie Nelson tapes; her witchiness, which my daughter adored;
her Picasso calendar; her physical prowess, which I said I could
not detail for young prudish minds; her love of my father's
crude, paunchy, dried out body which he displayed naked
around the house; her ignorance of math, blessed thing that
she didn't know what n stood for; and finally, my Grade 12
wonders, I said, I was marrying her because she was gorgeous.
I stopped talking and surveyed the class as it held its breath
and watched me, soundless, and then Maxine began to clap
and a few other girls joined in and finally the whole class
applauded, even James.

The bed arrived on a Saturday morning. Two men in blue
jumpsuits carried it up to the second floor while my father
watched from his commode in the foyer and brayed instructions. Jennifer and the kids came over for breakfast, a trial
run before they moved in the following Saturday. Jennifer
hung a few pictures and unpacked her tea set and then we sat
on the porch and ate toasted bagels while the kids romped on
the second floor. Lionel, the two-year-old, fell down the stairs
and broke a tooth and this initiated Jennifer's exodus, the
house suddenly silent as if caught in the eye of the storm.
Natalie wanted to get a cat before the onslaught and so I drove
her down to the Humane Society where we picked out a
skinny tabby. She was quiet during the drive home and when
I asked her if she was worried she said she wasn't and I chose
to believe her. I asked if we talked enough, about her school,

about what was important. She said she wasn't sure what was important but that I was a good father and she was glad I had stopped drinking because now she didn't have to hide bottles anymore. I looked over at her. She was looking straight ahead and when one of her eyebrows went up and down I thought of Holly in the dull grey light of the upstairs room. In the morning Natalie and I had breakfast on the porch, which looked out onto the street. She was holding her new cat and scratching its ears. The lilacs were blooming on the bush alongside the house and when the wind blew from the south the scent came in through the open kitchen window and filled the house and drifted out to where we were sitting. Jennifer phoned in the afternoon to say that Lionel was okay, it was just a baby tooth, and the family was in the midst of packing. Then she hesitated and asked, "Are you sure, do you want this?" I looked around as if she were standing behind me, then I came back to the phone and said, "Yes, yes, I do."

The next day in class Maxine Duras gave a presentation on the futility of studying math beyond Grade 10. She said that for other than purely aesthetic reasons, a tickling of the mind perhaps, imagination, or philosophy, there was no reason to do math. She asked, "Does it make me a better person?" She talked about Gulliver's voyage to Laputa where mathematicians are sleepy dreamers and bad tailors. She said, "The smallest circle hath as many degrees as the largest," and she flapped a bladder of pebbles for effect. I challenged Maxine, saying that even if mathematics was an abstract science, that didn't make it irrelevant. I asked her this: if you go to the dentist with a toothache does the dentist extract the toothache, which is the specific, or the tooth, which represents the general? She muttered something about the tooth and the toothache being inseparable but I waved her away and squeaked open my Thermos, and the squeak itself produced a sharp longing. I poured myself coffee, black, and standing there, poised on the brink of a lesson, I saw the path ahead of me as arduous and full of moments of sharp longing, and the students before me appeared as a large group standing off in the distance, generously holding up a bottle as if to share it. The image was quick and full of allure. It arrived through a glass, dimly.

Hungry

�֎

I'M ON MY bike near Sargent and this guy Patty is running his mouth off at me. He's wearing blue and his hands are in fists. He looks like my dog. His mouth is open. I tell Patty to shut up and he doesn't so I call on him and he says something about Tiff Trinkett and takes off down the street.

It's a good afternoon, my day off at the car wash, no afternoon classes, so I go past the school and sit on a curb. At three thirty Tiff comes out holding her books. She's with Jennifer. Jennifer's talking. Tiff's laughing. Then they're standing in front of me and I look up at them. There's a white cloud, like scissors, in the sky.

Tiff's got something written on her chest, close to her bare shoulder. It says, "Freak."

"What the fuck," I say.

She shrugs. Says Hazel wrote it. She scrubs at it with a fist.

We go to Subway. There's an old woman with blue shoes and a dirty coat. The old woman has her face in her coffee. Swings her short legs. Jennifer buys a sub and we go outside and share a drink. Jennifer says her brother got a job at Western Glove.

"Sewing jeans for little girl's asses," Tiff says.

"Fourteen bucks an hour," I say. Then I tell her that Patty was calling her down. Getting nasty.

"Prick," she says.

I know she knows Patty. They were together two months ago and then Patty's brother wanted in and Tiff ran. But I don't speak. Just smoke and look at the writing on her chest and I think about this time in Geo when we were doing the layers of the earth and I brought in a display made out of food. Graham crackers for the crust, raspberry Jell-O for the core, other kinds of Jell-O, sugar, margarine. I have always been intense about marks and projects and my father, happy to see this, cheerleads me in my schooling and he helped me build the Jell-O piece. So, I brought it in for a display and during the class we gobbled up the earth piece. Used plastic spoons and jiggled it off the plywood platter to our mouths. Mr. Harrison said it was great, just great. One hundred per cent. He shook my hand. Then he talked about the age of the world. He took out these soil samples and pointed at the layers and named them. Lots of hard words that sounded like he was stuttering or maybe trying out a poem.

"Mr. Davis," he said. "What's this?" He pointed at the middle sample, middle layer.

I said, "Dirt."

"No, no, no, no, Mr. Davis. It's both your past and your future." And he laughed. Then he passed around some black rocks that were sleeping on cotton inside little glass cubes. "Be careful,"

Mr. Harrison said. "These are four billion years old." He was terribly excited. And his voice went up and down, all music-like, and I didn't hear the words, only the sounds he made.

TIFF AND I LEAVE Jen and go to my place. It's a tiny green house behind the food bank. My father went into the food bank once and he came back with canned corn and scalloped potatoes in a box and a bag of rice. He didn't know what to do with the rice so I ended up using it for another project, music class, where I built a hollow instrument out of paste and newspaper and poured the rice inside.

My house smells like bacon and I know my father had a big lunch and then left for work. The clock in the kitchen is tearing along forty-five minutes ahead of real time. Wanda's there. He's sitting on the couch with Harry, my dog, and they're watching *Terminator*. Wanda showed up one day a couple of months ago. Just sitting on our couch eating chips. I asked him who he was and he mumbled something and then I asked him where he was from and he said Wanda. So, he's Wanda. Little black kid with a mother who works three jobs, and when he's home alone he's scared and so he hangs at our house.

"Hey, Wanda," Tiff says.

He looks up and then back at the TV.

"I saw your mom, Wanda," I say. "She's home. You can leave now."

He says he wants to finish the movie. I make him a peanut butter sandwich and tell him to go home. He gets up and shuffles sideways and then out the door.

I sit down and Tiff sits on my lap and says what she wants. Leather couches, a fifty-seven-inch HD Sony, a tight little foreign car and an espresso machine. She closes her eyes and dreams about a tiny white cup with foam spilling over it. She wants a pair of hipsters from Below the Belt. She keeps talking and her mouth twists when she gets greedy. "You getting a stick," she says. Then she kisses me. Her breath all over my face. Harry's lying on the floor, watching us.

She opens my jeans and goes, "Big stick." She has a shiny green thong and a red bra and looking at her I think, Christmas. So we fool around, but we don't do it. It makes her too sad when we do it. I have little tricks to change her mind, like I'm the cat and she's the mouse, but I haven't caught her for the last while. "C'mon, Sandy," she mumbles, and we float. After, we put our clothes back on and we sit on the couch and eat popcorn and watch TV.

When my older brother Jack comes home he looks at us on the couch and then he goes in the kitchen and fries some eggs. He steps back into the living room, holding his plate, his fork up in the air like a spear. He eats slowly, watching us watch TV.

Tiff swivels her head from Jack to the TV and back again.

"It's all good," I say.

"How are ya, Tiff?" my brother says.

Tiff sits up. Puts one hand up near her neck. "Good. Jack. Everything's good."

My brother nods. Then he tells me that the boys at Midtown want me to work tomorrow morning.

"I got school," I say.

"That so."

He asks Tiff where I was today.

She doesn't know. She looks at me with her wet eyes and says, "At school?"

"Yeah," I say. And I tell Jack about Mr. Harrison and the soil samples. About the Jell-O and graham crackers, which isn't really true, because it happened two months ago.

When I'm done, my brother nods and says, "You're such a loser."

AT MIDTOWN, I VACUUM. Two minutes to do the front and back, shake out the mats, clean the trunk, and put everything back together. If I'm too slow, I lose a buck a car. If Earl finds gravel under the mats when he's wiping down the inside with Armor All, he takes another dollar. Six o'clock we get a fifteen-minute break and I smoke two and a half cigarettes and listen to the boys talk. They think I'm shit. Jack's little brother, a cracker.

By the second month Earl's still beating on me. He calls me down, or hits me with the broom and the gang laughs and then they all turn away. I'm bigger than him but he's got his buddies, and so I always walk away. One afternoon, he catches me coming out of the can and he gets stupid and says, "What up you think you're solid then come fight me."

I laugh.

He spits and says, "Let's go."

I say, "I don't care." I throw my hat on the ground and hit him first, knowing that surprise is everything and it is. I give him a few more good shots and with each one his eyes open, like he's waking up and he doesn't know where he is. I leave him sitting on the ground, leaning against the garage door. His hands are flat on the ground, like he's trying to stop himself from falling through a hole. After that day, Earl leaves me alone. I settle into work and I'm free. Nobody's on me and I fall in love with the tang of the cars. You open the door and wham, it's handsome, smelling like the lawyer woman who stands at attention in the sunshine, talking talking talking on her silver phone, hand swaying at her hip. Oh man. Sometimes, when it's slow, I push my nose against the leather and breathe deep and think about Tiff and me rollin'. Still, it's a shit job, but the money's good, and it keeps me away from Jack in the evenings. I tell Tiff never to go over to my place on her own. Jack's a scrub, I say.

MR. HARRISON TAKES the Geo class to his house one day after school. It's a big house with a sunken living room and leather couches and we sit there and watch slides of his trip to a place called Machu Picchu. There's a slide of Mr. Harrison standing by some ruins with his wife and daughter and they both look good. They're smiling, the daughter is blonde and she has great legs, and Mrs. Harrison has green shorts, and Mr. Harrison is wearing binoculars and a grey hat with a wide rim and he's pointing off at something behind the person taking the photo. Then there's a shot of Mr. Harrison in a Speedo on a beach and we all laugh and make fun of him. Later, he brings out food, little bits of quiche, and wieners wrapped in dough, and taco chips and punch. Outside, beyond the picture window, there's a pool. I go to the bathroom. It's painted dark red and the towels are rusty coloured and soft and the Jacuzzi is red. On the cabinet there's a bowl. It's copper inside and black outside and on the bottom it says Burma. I put it in my jacket pocket and then go back to the sunken living room where Mr. Harrison is talking about deep sea fishing and taking Gravol for seasickness and sleeping through the whole expedition. He says the word *expedition* carefully, as if it were a word with a lot of meaning.

I get home late and walk in the door and I can hear the snap of something, very regular, a crack and then a sharp spitting sound, like a whip. Then I hear Jack laugh and a girl's voice goes "Oh, oh, Jesus," and I know it's Tiff by the way the 'us' in Jesus goes up and up. They're in the living room. Wanda's there too. He's standing against the wall, his head really black against the light paint, and his eyes are wide open. Jack is standing across the room and he's holding a pellet gun that's been shortened and he's aiming at Wanda. He fires, the pellet hits the wall just above Wanda's right shoulder, Tiff squeals and claps, and Jack, when he sees me, touches the barrel to his chest. "Fucking circus," he says. "And I'm the ringmaster."

I ask Wanda if he's okay. He grins. Yeah, he's all good.

"Just his head left," Jack says.

I tell him to stop.

"Whoaa," Jack says. "Whoaa." And he raises the barrel and pulls the trigger and the pellet enters Wanda's left eye and Wanda doesn't shift, doesn't say anything, just puts his hand up to touch his face, as if he were checking for something. His mouth opens and closes, but no sound comes out. Tiff moves around the room, arms in the air, lost in the music.

I go to Wanda and say, "Hey, you okay?"

He nods. Shrugs. His mouth moves, but still there's no sound.

"Here." I take his hand away from his eye. No blood. This is good. Blood means damage. His eyeball is whacked though. Out of control, like a marble in a bowl.

I hold up two fingers. "Look here," I say.

His eye rolls left and all that remains is a white ping-pong ball. He sighs and lays his head against my shoulder.

"Fuck," I say. I sit him on the couch and go to the kitchen for a rag and some water. When I come back Jack is going, "It's cool. No problem, Wanda. Everything's cool."

There's the tiniest trickle of blood coming out of the corner of Wanda's eye. I dab at it. My hands are shaking.

Jack says, "He'll be good. The bullet bounced off."

"Uh-uh," I say. "It's fuckin' in his head."

"Don't think so. Maybe it went through." Jack touches the back of Wanda's head. "Did it?"

Wanda looks up at Jack. His good eye is big, almost happy. "Hungry," he says.

"There ya go," Jack says. "You're hungry. What'll ya have. Pizza Pop? Cheerios? Ice cream?"

"Hungry," Wanda says.

"Shut up with the fucking music, will ya?" Jack waves a hand at Tiff, who slides across the room and stands with her back against the wall, right where Wanda got hit. She smiles sleepily.

I take Wanda's hand and pull him up. "Here." I pull him towards the door and he follows easily. Nothing wrong with his walking.

"Where ya going?" Jack's voice is hard.

I don't answer, just take Wanda's arm and lead him outside and down the stairs onto the sidewalk and we go up together to Notre Dame and stand at the bus stop in the darkness.

"I'm gonna take you to the hospital, Wanda, okay?"

He's holding an orange towel to his hurt eye and so I can only see one side of his face and that side twists up and he grunts and he sounds like Harry when he's sad or wants petting. So I pat Wanda's curly head and say, "You're good, man. All good."

"Hungry," he says.

"I know. I know. Me too."

He says it again, "Hungry," and then we're on the bus, sitting near the back, and the word keeps jumping out of his mouth.

"Hungry."

"Hungry."

"Hungry."

The people on the bus are watching. They're disgusted by this chanting noise and so I turn away from Wanda and pretend that I am not his.

WE GO TO CHILDREN'S, where the nurses do their serious look thing and one nurse, fat in blue pants that are too short, asks a bagful of questions while Wanda sits there dying. Then I am alone in a room. A stethoscope and a white coat on the door. There are all these beautiful clean objects on the desk. Beakers, sticks, cotton balls, a little black bed with paper laid out over it in case you're bleeding and shit. A poster on the wall showing pink lungs and black lungs and at that point I want a cigarette.

The door opens and in comes a thin nurse. She's holding a chart. Her arms are bare. She's got a great ass. I can tell because her green fatigues or whatever you call them are tight and show off the hollows at her bum. She's married, or something. A ring and she smells like bath powder and her hands are older like she's done dishes a lot, or maybe changed diapers. I can smell her goodness and I think what it would be like to be married to her.

She sits close and says that Wanda's hurt bad. He can't talk, so I'll have to talk for him.

"Hungry," she says. "What's that?"

A cloud opens above me. The thin nurse is with me in a large house, twenty-five rooms at least, and we are sitting by the pool drinking cognac out of sniffers. She is leaning into me and her mouth opens and she talks softly.

"Can you tell me his name?" she asks.

I shake my head.

"Hungry. He keeps saying that."

She is wearing nothing. I am wearing nothing. The pool has green lights. The cognac is making her voice slow down. "Do you know his name?"

"I don't know him. He got hurt, I found him, I brought him here."

Her eyes are the colour of the pool.

"Whose gun was it?"

"I dunno."

"So, you found him and brought him here like the Good Samaritan."

"I don't know what you're talking about."

My wife holds up her long fingers and shows me the lines in her palms. "Where do you live?"

I give her Mr. Harrison's address and make up a phone number. Then someone turns out the green lights, and the pool and the twenty-five rooms and the oily cognac all disappear and my wife sits up and says, "Good." Then the fat nurse leans into the room and makes a soft noise and the thin nurse stands and leaves and I am alone. For five minutes I sit and wait and nothing happens, no one comes back, and when I step out into the hall it is silent and empty, and it's like everyone has died, the thin nurse, Wanda, the fat nurse, the woman at the desk, and I turn and follow the green line down past the elevators, past the security guard, out the exit, and into the night.

WHEN I GET HOME, I enter through the back door and I can hear loud music and voices and when I come through the kitchen door I see Tiff naked and sitting on my brother's lap and he's naked too. They're both facing the TV and Jack's hands come around Tiff's front and hold her tits. She's singing or something and he's singing too. They don't see me. They're on the couch and I can see them from behind and the side. I watch and then step back into the kitchen. The cast-iron frying pan is on the stove, the one my father uses to fry his pickerel and bacon. I pick it up. Mr. Fox, the Phys Ed teacher, taught us just last week the rich kid's game, tennis, how you're supposed to keep your arm straight as you swing through and hit the ball. In the kitchen I take a few practice swings with the frying pan. Then I go into the living room and aim at my brother's head. I lock my elbow and say, "I saved your ass." He looks up and back to find my words and he sees me. His eyes are like two yellow balls of surprise, and just as he's about to call out, I follow through with this mad swing that Mr. Fox'd be terrifically proud of, and I catch one of those balls dead centre, and I can feel it, a perfect hit, and I know it's a winner.

Never Too Late

THE DOG SHOWED up at his ranch on a cool morning in April, two days after a spring blizzard blew in off the Rockies, leaving a foot of snow and trapping cows and calves in the gulches of the south section. When he stepped out onto the porch, the dog was waiting for him.

"Who're you?" he asked. Sad eyes. Black. Curls like it'd just come from having a perm.

He stepped around the dog and walked out to the barn, lifted the latch, swung the door, and stepped inside. The dog slipped through the door.

The stable was in shadows. Warm. The smell of hay and horse and manure.

He saddled Blue and slipped on the bit while the dog sat and watched. He guided the horse out into the yard. Steam from his nostrils. A quick sideways movement. He swung up in the saddle and set out for the south pasture. The dog followed.

Three hours and one dead calf later he stabled and curried Blue, walked outside, closed the barn door, and walked out to his pickup. He lowered the rear gate and the dog scrambled up into the bed. He shut the gate.

"Don't talk much, do you?" he said.

He climbed into the pickup and drove to town and parked in front of Lachlan's. The dog jumped out of the box and followed him into the clinic. He approached the front desk and said, "Hi Julie."

Julie looked up at him with her clear blue eyes. "Hi Bev."

"Bit of a storm we had," he said.

"Was. My man was stranded in Calgary for two nights. Got in at five this morning. Said the ditches were full of cars emptied of all their fools." She grinned. The deepest dimples.

"Lachlan around?"

"He's out. Calving season, as you know."

"I do." Bev turned and looked down at the dog. "This here girl found me this morning and won't let me go. Like Lepages."

Julie rose and bent over the desk for a closer look. "That one belongs to Janice Collicutt. Curly Coated Retriever. Spayed her last year. She's a runner. And a mute."

"That a fact."

"It is. Born without a voice. Except when she smells smoke. Then she howls like all get-out."

"Well, I'm not a smoker."

"Good thing then. You'll want to find Janice."

"I do."

"She lives at Alton Manor. Janice will be happy to see her dog. She loses her at least once a week."

"Might want to tie her up."

"Oh, she wouldn't do that. She's too kind-hearted. She needs a good trainer."

He took note of Julie's dimples one last time and then turned to go.

"Careful on the roads," she said.

"Sun's out. Ice is melting."

"Still."

As he loaded the dog in the bed, he wondered what the mutt was called. Curly, he supposed. He drove to Alton Manor and parked in the loading zone. He put on his hazards and walked up the sidewalk to the front door. In the lobby there was an intercom and a list of names and numbers. He found Collicutt, Janice, and punched in 542. A sign on the glass door read, NO PETS ALLOWED. The ringer went off six times before a woman answered.

"Who's that?"

"My name's Bev. I have your dog."

"Keller? You found her?"

"She found me."

"Where then?"

"On my ranch. Sitting on the porch."

"Oh my."

"Should I come up?"

The buzzer rang to free the lock and Bev stared at it, and then pulled the handle and entered. He took the elevator to the fifth floor, patting Keller on the head. "Atta girl," he said. "You're going home."

When the door opened he was surprised by a number of things. Janice Collicutt was in an electric wheelchair, and her face was too smooth and unlined and young for her to be living in an old folk's home, and her hair was curly like her dog's, and she had a green eye and a brown eye, and she was a looker.

Keller entered, sniffed the wheels of the chair, and lay down in the middle of the living room.

Janice spun around and turned left and disappeared. "Come in," she called. "In here. Sit down."

She was parked at the table, eating plain macaroni and ketchup.

He sat. Looked around. The dishes needed washing.

"I suppose you're looking for a reward?" Janice said. "I can't do that. Keller would break the bank. I can offer you noodles though. You hungry?"

He was. "I'm fine," he said.

"Course you're fine." She motioned at the pot on the stove. "Help yourself."

He stood and took a bowl from the cabinet and spooned himself some macaroni and sat and squeezed a little ketchup into the bowl.

As they ate, Janice told him about her life. She lived at Alton Manor because it had elevators and wheelchair accessibility and because she was surrounded by other people. They might be a lot older, but they were good company. She said that she had multiple sclerosis. Five years earlier she'd begun to drop things, knives, pencils, her wallet, and then her left leg began to drag behind her as she walked and one day, lo and behold, she couldn't walk at all, and now here she was in a wheelchair. "My husband, Jack, walked away from me as soon as he found out about the MS. Cripples frighten him. He's remarried. Has a baby on the way. Thing is, he still thinks he owns me. I have an inheritance, from my father, and Jack thinks he should get some. Courts think differently." She ate some more. "What 'bout you?"

"What about me?"

"Your life. What do you do?"

"I have a ranch. Four hundred head of cattle. Horses."

She nodded. "Married?"

He shook his head.

"Been?"

"Once. A long time ago."

"I thought so. You have that look."

"What's that?"

"The look of a bachelor. A little forlorn. Threadbare."

"Is that right?"

"What I miss is the sex. Oh, of course, you don't have to be married to have sex, but it's easier. But then it turns humdrum."

He looked down at his empty bowl.

"People think because I'm in a wheelchair, I can't have sex. Not true."

Bev took up his hat and placed it on his head. He rose. "Nice meeting you, Miss Collicutt. You might want to watch your dog more carefully."

"I try. But she has to do her business and she gets loose and I can't chase her down. She gets excited about the big world out there. How far you from town?"

"Six miles."

"One time she ended up on a ranch fifty miles from here. They kept her for the winter. Saved me feeding her. You want her?"

"I favour cats."

"Keller's a pointer and a hunting dog. Needs some training though."

"That's probably true." He touched his hat. "Well. Goodbye."

"Yes. See you."

He didn't think so. All that talk of sex. He wondered if the sickness had addled her brain. Driving home, he kept thinking about her eyes, the brightness there in two different colours.

ON WEDNESDAY, as was the case every other week, he filled in as the auctioneer at the livestock sale in town. Gone were the heady times of day-long sales and thousands of head of cattle. What arrived these days was a worn-out dairy cow sold by a single owner, a bull with nothing in his rocket, or a small bevy of heifers bought up by a buyer from Monsanto. The auction lasted two hours. Bev caught sight of Janice sitting in her wheelchair along the walkway above the pen. He saw her at the exact moment a bony Jersey cow entered the ring. He said, "Ain't she a sweetheart," and he sold her for five dollars.

Later, Janice was waiting for him in the parking lot. He feigned delight or perhaps he wasn't feigning at all. He said, "Nice to see you Miss Collicutt," and she said, "Janice."

Then she said, "What's gonna happen to that sweetheart of a dairy cow?"

"Well," he said, "She'll be turned into glue."

"That's sad," she said.

He took off his hat. "Never thought of it that way." He looked around. "How did you get here?"

"I rode my chair."

"On the highway."

"Yes."

"Would you like a lift back?"

"I would," she said. And then she said his name, "Bev."

As he helped her into the cab of his pickup he was aware of her arm around his neck and how her chest pushed against his ribs and he was aware too of how loose and floppy her left leg was. He found several two-by-tens beside the feedlot and used those as planks to drive the wheelchair into the bed of the truck. Threw the planks in alongside. Janice was tickled pink to see all the trouble he went to. When he dropped her off and settled her back into her chair, she touched his arm and said, "You might want to hold onto those planks. Just in case."

The following evening, a Thursday, he arranged to pick her up and take her out for steak in Calgary. They drove up the Number 2 highway and found a Keg on the south side of the city. As they entered the restaurant he wondered if he could get used to being with a woman who wasn't able to ride or rope or wrangle, a woman whose head would always only reach the height of his belt buckle.

She ordered a Silver Cloud and a sirloin medium rare and mushrooms on the side. She said, "You're not particular. I like that."

"Not sure what you mean by that."

"Not squeamish."

He lifted an eyebrow.

"You're not put off by a gimp."

"Never crossed my mind," he said.

"You see. That's what I mean. I tried Internet dating once, just for a month, and you should see the freaks that come crawling out from under the rug. One fellow wanted me to sit naked in my chair while he satisfied himself. I sent him home."

"Sounds dangerous," he said.

"Not really. These are very weak men. Morally. They have no backbone." She watched him carefully. "Am I too blunt?"

"You are blunt. Too? I wouldn't say."

"I frightened you the other day, talking about sex."

He smiled. "And now you're talking about it again."

"I don't have a lot of time left. Maybe a year. All the old rules have been chucked out."

The food arrived. "Would you cut my steak?" she asked, and pushed her plate towards him. He cut it for her and thought of children.

He said, "I couldn't have babies. That's why Dorothy left me."

"I never wanted babies. Too old anyways."

"That's not what I'm saying. I'm just trying to be honest."

"I knew who you were the moment we met."

"Yeah? Did you know I'm celibate?"

"That a threat?" She laughed.

"I'm a Christian as well."

"Makes sense."

"How 'bout you?"

"I could be if it's useful."

"This isn't a negotiation. It's about faith."

"I know all that."

Driving home there was a deep silence that didn't feel like silence because he sensed her breathing and her movements and at one point she reached out her strong hand, her left, and stroked his head and then ran it down to his neck. It was shocking to feel once again a woman's touch.

"Could I spend the night at your place?" she asked. "I get tired of my apartment."

"I only have one bed," he said.

"Perfect."

"What would we do with the wheelchair?"

"Put it in the barn with the horses," she said. "You can carry me inside."

He was quiet.

"You think too much," she said.

"Think so?"

"This isn't life or death," she said. She took her phone out of her purse and entered a number. He heard her talking, saying that her door was open and that Keller needed water and food and she needed to go outside. "Don't let her off the leash," she said. "She'll run."

BEV HAD NOT had sex with a woman for twenty years, two months and three days, not as if anyone was keeping track. The last woman he'd slept with was his ex-wife Dorothy, who left him after years of trying to have children. The doctors determined that he was at fault, perhaps because of his acquaintance with Agent Orange during his tour of duty in Vietnam. When Dorothy left him she claimed to be heartbroken. And then she married a town man, manager of the Credit Union, who gave her three children. Bev saw them in church, sitting five abreast, all clean and wonderful and contented. He was happy for Dorothy, and this was his greatest problem, that he imagined happiness was found elsewhere, certainly not in his own home and heart.

The previous fall he'd driven to IKEA in Calgary and picked up kitchen cabinets and then gone home and installed them, laying out the boxes and reading the instructions, assembling the cabinets and then hanging them. Making love to Janice Collicutt was like putting together an IKEA kitchen, only in this case the instructions came from Janice herself, telling him to move her leg just so, to adjust his weight, and to help her hand find his cock. Sex with Janice was surprising for its mechanics. There were no tricks, there was no hesitation, everything fell together just so.

At night, he woke to find that Janice's left leg had clamped him to the bed and held him with a ferocious possession. He lifted her leg and slid out of bed and walked naked into the kitchen and ran a cold glass of water. Drank it looking out at his yard and the pickup and the single yard light that fell like a sharp sun across the barn that held his three horses and a few layers and housed a motorized wheelchair. What was he doing? He laid the glass upside down in the sink and went back to bed and dreamed of a talking dog.

IN THE EARLY morning, as Janice slept, he stepped out onto his porch and looked at the foothills to the west. They were not grand compared to the Rockies beyond, but they were a stepping stone to something greater, and he saw himself stepping into a new life, and the mountains dwarfed him and the foothills were miles away, and the sun rising behind him seemed just as happy for him as he was, in fact the sun seemed to wink at him. As a young man he had suffered anger and fits of rage and he had fought anything and everything that was presented before him. This all stopped one day. It had been immediate and true. A real conversion. He had been out riding fence, leaning into a westerly, fighting the snow and cold, and he'd gotten off to splice the fence when the barbwire snapped and wrapped around his neck and threw him to the ground. He would have bled out if his horse hadn't nuzzled him out of the drifts and walked him home. On the horse, leaning forward, his face pressed against the mane, he'd had a vision of himself travelling down a wide road towards a bright light, and it was that bright light that stayed with him. From that day, he stopped all fighting, rid himself of his rage, forgave Dorothy, forgave himself, and he got himself a cat, an animal he'd always disliked. He grew to love the cat, a fat calico that proved to be a tremendous mouser. He was a changed man—still resolute, with little patience for fools, but kinder, softer, and sometimes leaning towards tears.

HE SAW HER seven days in a row. He'd drive over to her apartment late in the day and roust her and wheel her out to his pickup and place her in the cab and drive the wheelchair up the planks into the box and then climb in beside her, and each time he did so he was delirious. He'd take a deep breath and then say, "Here we go." And she'd grin and adjust her loose body and answer, "Yes." They'd drive the roads below the foothills, watching the light fade pink and then dark green and then dusty grey and finally a soft blackness that verged on purple, which meant that the mountains were catching the last of the sun on their backsides. She was a bigger talker than he was. She'd grown up in town and been wooed by various men from a young age, perhaps because her father had money, or maybe because her eyes were different colours. "Men seem to like that," she said. Her father had made his money selling mud to drilling companies. "A mud millionaire is what he calls himself." He'd bought her a house after her divorce, and offered her a full-time nurse, but she preferred the company of the tenants at the Alton. "A lot of wisdom there, along with some unwanted advice," she said. "My father flew me to Italy last year for that operation that opens the jugular venous system. That Zamboni guy discovered it. For a month I was leaping about like a newborn colt. And then, bang, I lost feeling in my leg and arm and I was back in a wheelchair." She talked about herself as if she were describing someone else. Like she was watching her reflection in a triple-glazed window. And always, when darkness had arrived completely, he would drive her to his house and carry her inside and drop her on the bed and undress her and then take off his own clothes and lie down beside her and they would make love. One time, he discovered that he was crying, and she wiped at his tears and said that he was the sweetest thing she'd ever known. He said that with age his tears came more easily, and though it embarrassed him to admit this, he said it anyway.

For twenty years he had forsaken women and had even denied thoughts of sex. Like a monk who is faithful, he had cleansed himself. And now Janice was in his life and he had tumbled down the hill of virtue into the slough of carnality and he had never felt so free and so liberated and so full of life. She was beautiful and yet she wasn't. He wanted to tell someone about her and one afternoon at a café just outside Calgary, when the waitress told him that he had a glint in his eye, he agreed and said he'd just met the love of his life. "It's never too late I guess," the waitress said, and he saw that she was calling him both old and lucky. He couldn't argue with that.

ON A FRIDAY MORNING, after eating fried potatoes and eggs with Janice, he dropped her off at the Alton and he went to see Harv Engel, the manager of the Credit Union, the same man who had married and promptly seeded Bev's ex-wife.

Harv was a big man. Some might have called him fat. He liked to say things like, "Let me be frank," or, "Let's cut to the chase," or, "You need to line up your ducks." Harv was in his office, holding down his chair. He was breathing heavily, as if he had run a long distance to meet with Bev. He sighed and said, "Let me be frank. I've cut you slack for the past year, reducing your interest rates, forgoing payments, but the time has come to face the music. You either sell the ranch or declare bankruptcy. Selling seems the better option."

Here was a dreary flannel-mouthed barrel of a man who soaked up numbers and spat them back at you as if the numbers themselves were the only truth in the world.

Bev crossed his legs, laid his cowboy hat on his lap, and laid out a few numbers himself. "Give me sixty days," he said. "May 30th. I'll have the thirty thousand."

"Where you gonna get that much money in that time, Bev? I hate to say this, but we can't afford to keep postponing the inevitable. The feedlot's looking for a new manager. They could use a good man like you."

"Aww, heck, I'm too old to start all over again. And I can't live in town, Harv. It'd kill me."

"Ranch is killing you, Bev. Maybe there's a little house in the country you could rent. I'll keep my ear to the ground." He touched an earlobe as he spoke, and Bev was aware of how his head was like a 20-gallon barrel sitting atop the 45-gallon drum that was his body.

"How are the kids?" Bev asked.

"Fine. Fine. Crystal's playing volleyball this year. She has Dorothy's legs. A real jumper."

"Say hi to Dorothy."

"For sure. For sure." They shook hands. "Give the feedlot a call," he said.

He drove home slowly taking the back roads, windows open, wondering if he was an ignoramus. He dismissed this thought and watched two geese, wings reared, land on the grassland.

At home, he discovered a Cadillac in his yard, parked near the barn. Jack Collicutt climbed out. Bev sat in the pickup and watched Jack approach. Rolled down the window.

"Mr. Wohlgemuht?"

"That's me," Bev said.

Jack stopped a few yards from the pickup. "Stay away from Janice," he said. "She's not terribly clear these days and is easily influenced."

Bev waited. When nothing more was offered he said, "That it?"

"I think that'd be enough."

"Last I heard you were married to another woman. Makes no sense why you should be concerned with Janice."

"Like I said, she's not at the top of her game. I'm concerned that you're after more than Janice."

"I'm not after anything, Mr. Collicutt. You can climb back into your slick car and get off my property."

Jack looked around. "Tittle-tattle tells me it isn't your property much longer."

Bev opened the pickup door and stepped out. Jack moved backwards, palms held out, and then turned and scattered back to his shiny car.

Over the next three days, Bev and a neighbour boy who was all arms and acne rounded up bull calves and together they branded and inoculated and castrated. The skies were clear, the sun shone, the world was endless. During that time, Janice left him three messages that he didn't reply to. He told himself that he was tired, that his ranch was demanding his time, but he knew that Jack's visit had surprised him. He now saw himself as Jack Collicutt saw him—a bankrupt rancher who had fallen into the arms of a wealthy divorcee. It wasn't a pretty thought. One night, late, the phone rang and he picked it up. Janice's voice was soft and happy.

"There you are," she said, as if they had been playing hide and seek.

"Yup."

"What are you doing?"

"Soaking in the tub."

"Nice. I miss you."

"Well."

"You wanna come over?"

"I'm naked as night."

"Get dressed, come by, and get naked again."

"I don't know. I sort of fell off the path and I'm not sure it did me any good."

"Good? What garbage."

"You don't know me at all," he said.

"I know more than you think I know."

"Well, put it this way then. I'd rather you didn't know all that I think you don't know." He paused. "What do you know?"

"That you're about to lose the ranch."

"There a sign on my back or something?"

"Jack told me."

"He informed me of the same."

"You talked to Jack?"

"He paid me a visit. Warned me to stay away from you."

"And you're going to obey him? Get over here, Bev." She hung up.

He climbed from the tub and shaved, angling his head to catch the dim light above the bathroom mirror. Splashed on aftershave. Dressed. Donned his white suede Sheplers. Stepped outside and smelled the air. A warm wind was blowing from the south. The stars were completely hung.

GOING ON 3 A.M. they were still talking. He'd told her everything vital about himself. His time in the mental hospital after his tour in Vietnam, the death of his father and mother and how much he missed his mother, his barren marriage, his unkindness to Dorothy when he learned that he was to blame for the lack of children, the money shortage, and his discovery early on in life that hard work kept him sane, even if that same hard work failed to provide him with the means to hang on to the little that he had. He said that he lacked generosity. In love, in life, and even with himself. He paused, suddenly shy. He had never before spoken so clearly of himself, and his honesty surprised him, and the words and what they meant surprised him as well. He was like the man who wakes from a deep sleep and looks down at his feet and only comes to recognize those feet as his own by addressing them.

They were lying side by side in Janice's bed. Janice held his hand as he spoke and when he was finished she said, "You're way too hard on yourself."

"I might disagree."

"Not very bright then, are you?" She maneuvered her body on top of his. "Help me here," she said, and he lifted and pulled until she had settled. Her weight was lovely. Her mouth was strong. Her generous heart.

THE FOLLOWING NIGHT, alone in his own bed, he dreamed of a dog howling and he woke from a sinister sleep and heard the howling in his yard. He walked naked to the front door and opened it to discover Keller in the driveway howling at the fire that was consuming his stable. He ran for the barn. Blue was circling his pen, snorting and quivering. He laid a gunnysack over his eyes and led Blue out and set him free. He fetched the two remaining horses and then stood at a distance and felt the heat on his face and crotch and arms and he watched the sparks tear off into the night and he listened to the chickens burn. No use in calling the volunteer fire department.

He made sure no sparks came near the house. At some point he dressed and made himself a cup of coffee and sat on the stoop with Keller and together they watched the roof cave in. An unholy sound. Keller emitted a forlorn howl. Alley, his calico, appeared and walked a figure eight between his legs. He rubbed her ears. Jonesy, the neighbour to the south, drove up in his pickup and climbed out and asked about the livestock.

"Lost a few chickens. I freed the horses." Bev waved a hand out towards the road indicating the direction they'd run.

Jonesy rested a boot on the steps. "Any idea how it started?"

"Well, horses don't start fires."

"Perhaps electrical," Jonesy said.

"Perhaps."

"You don't think so."

"No. I don't."

"I doubt it too." Jonesy went inside and came back out with a coffee. "You have enemies?"

"The bank?"

Jonesy lifted an eyebrow.

THE INSURANCE MAN showed up the following day. He'd dragged along a fire inspector from Calgary and the two of them spent the afternoon going through the rubble. Bev watched them from the kitchen window as they walked in rubber boots around the remnants of the barn. A neighbour five miles east had rounded up his horses and delivered them. He'd put them out to pasture where they were now, standing with their rumps against a cold wind. He made coffee, poured two mugs, and carried them out to the men.

"Don't know if you take cream or sugar," he said.

"Black's fine," said the fire inspector. The insurance man, a thin fellow who when he spoke sounded as if he had stones in his mouth, said that he didn't drink coffee any which way, thanks. And so Bev, who wasn't given to waste, took it for himself.

According to the inspector the fire was the result of arson. "Scorch marks indicate an accelerant was used." When he spoke he looked at the sky, and because this was so, Bev felt that he was guilty of something.

The insurance man said it would take a while to process the claim. "Police and such will have to be involved," he said past the stones. Unlike the fire inspector, he looked directly at Bev as he spoke. Bev didn't turn away.

"How'd you get the horses out in time?" the insurance man asked.

"Dog woke me."

"Yeah? I didn't see a dog."

"She's a runner. Belongs to a woman I know. She happened to show up last night and went all apeshit. Doesn't like the smell of smoke."

"Lucky then," the insurance man said. He had a name, but Bev had forgotten it. "Fact is, it all seems terribly convenient, you with money troubles and all."

"Where'd you get that?"

"My business to know."

Bev said, "If it'd been me set that fire I'd have burned the house down."

The fire inspector thought this was humorous. The insurance man didn't. Truth was, Bev hadn't intended to be funny. He was being honest.

He was eager to get his hands on Jack Collicutt, and in his earlier days, when he had been impetuous and full of rage, he would have paid him a visit at his high-school office and threatened him with a branding. Or worse. As it was, he stayed put. He rode Blue bareback out along the south pasture. Vs of geese flew overhead. A great horned owl sat a fence post.

In the early evening she called. "I heard," she said.

"That's quite a dog you have."

"Isn't she?"

"And quite a man you were married to."

"I'm so sorry," she said.

"Well, *you* didn't burn the barn down."

"You in trouble?"

"Might be." It was quiet, then he said, "Nothing I can't handle."

"You like being a loner, don't you?"

"A lot less trouble."

"Yeah, people are no fun, are they."

"Most."

"I can help out. It'd please me."

"Wouldn't please *me*," he said.

"'Course not. You're a big proud rancher. If it helps, you can pay me back. Or count it as a reward for finding Keller. Who's still out there somewheres."

"Engel, and everybody else, they'd see me as your whore."

"That's pure mean," she said.

"Where can this go? Your ex-husband's a madman, your dog's out of control, and I've got these two by tens in the bed of my pickup reminding me you won't be around much longer."

"'Course I'll die. Maybe be dead next year. But right now I'm here. Here I am."

"You lookin' to get married?"

"For sure not. Marriage kills your sex life."

"What do you want then?"

"Nothing, Bev. Might surprise you, but I want nothing. I'm happy. You gotta figure out what you're afraid of."

He sat on the couch before a black TV screen and saw there the faintest reflection of himself. He'd known outright physical terror and fear before and he knew the feeling it evoked, but this was different. This fear was like a heavy ache, and yet there were moments when if he turned his thoughts a certain way, the fear became a peaceful happiness and he was full of a bright light. It was like flipping a coin that offered two extremes.

And what would Janice say to this? Garbage.

He slept poorly. Kept waking, thinking he could hear her scratching at the door. And he rose to check the night, standing naked on the porch in the cold, looking over at the black carcass of the barn. A few times he called out, thinking she might be out there, but she didn't come.

In the morning, in the first pink light, she was waiting for him on the porch.

Saved

�֍

1.

THE LIEUTENANT'S OFFICE was dimly lit. There was a glass of water on the desk and a large seashell that was an ashtray, and a telephone and one pencil, perfectly sharp. The lieutenant walked around the room, smoking, touching the desk as he passed by it. Once, he lifted the pencil and then put it down again and he began to talk about the girl. He said that the death of a foreigner was never a good thing for him. He said that the error of her death might lie with the girl herself, with her own foolishness. Perhaps she did not know how to swim, or perhaps she wanted to die—this sometimes happened. The lieutenant said that the girl's death was a mystery, and he did not like mysteries. He liked to know the truth. He paused, lit another cigarette, and said, "You know this girl."

The boy shook his head.

"You went to her house."

"Not yet."

The lieutenant stepped forward quickly and struck the boy with an open hand to his head. To an onlooker it might have appeared that the lieutenant was striking the dust from a cushion. The boy did not react, though his head moved slightly.

"How many times did you go to her house?" the lieutenant asked.

"Once. She fed me."

"She fed me." The lieutenant repeated the words as if some meaning could be gleaned from them. He said, "You did not know her, yet she fed you."

The boy was frightened but he did not show it. He knew that because he was sitting in this lieutenant's office, and because a man who had much power was questioning him, for these reasons he was in trouble. He understood that he might not ever leave the building. He understood that his own death might be imminent. Even so, knowing all of this, he showed no fear. He said that the girl had had friends and the friends had invited him to eat because he was hungry.

"What did you eat?"

"I don't remember."

The lieutenant said that he would give the boy time to remember.

The boy thought about this and then he said, "Bread. And cheese."

The lieutenant said that he did not like cheese and those people who ate cheese smelled like goats. "Do you like cheese?" he asked. And then, not waiting for an answer, he went to his desk and picked up the pencil, opened a drawer, took a pad of paper, and began to write. He wrote with his left hand. He leaned on the desk and wrote carefully for a long time. When he straightened, he said, "On Tuesday you saw her."

The boy said no.

The lieutenant said, "You saw her and together you rode up to Monkey Mountain and then went down to the beach and she took off her clothes and she had on a bathing suit. What colour was the bathing suit?"

The boy said that he did not know the colour. "I was not there," he said.

The lieutenant put down the pencil and walked over to the boy and he took the boy's neck in his left hand and he squeezed and leaned forward and whispered, "The bathing suit was blue."

The boy saw pain. It entered the back of his head, passed by the backs of his eyes, and came out of his mouth.

The lieutenant stepped back. He said that the boy should not think he was an equal. Neither to the lieutenant, nor to the girl. "She was beautiful," he said. Even when she was dead. "Did you touch her?" he asked.

The boy stared at the floor. He did not answer. He saw the lieutenant's boots. The toes were round and scuffed. They needed polishing. The boy was good at polishing shoes. When he was younger, seven or eight, he had worked the corner near the post office on Bach Dang. Perhaps he had even polished this lieutenant's shoes.

The lieutenant began to speak again. He said that there were many unfortunate things in the world and one of these was the death of a nineteen-year-old American girl in his city, here in this country. And another was that a fifteen-year-old boy, who claimed to know nothing and who would be missed by no one should he disappear for some reason, might think that he could hold in his hands the sun, the moon and the stars.

The lieutenant spat.

He pulled up a chair and faced the boy. The boy did not look at him. The lieutenant said, "There was a bump." He touched the back of the boy's head. "Here." The hand came away and the lieutenant leaned backwards and raised his hands. "Where did this bump come from? Do we think that it grew there on its own? Like an onion would grow in the ground?" He shrugged. "Perhaps."

It was quiet. Outside, beyond the closed window, the boy heard the faint sound of motorcycles on the street. He thought about the street and the light that fell from above and how he might not see that light again.

"Her name," the lieutenant said.

The boy looked up. He looked past the lieutenant's face and he said, "That day, when I ate cheese, on that day she was called Marcie."

The lieutenant nodded. "On that day," he said. Then he sighed and said that the girl's friends had gone back to America. They had taken the girl's body with them. So now, there was nothing more.

The lieutenant sat up straight and said, "They talked too much." He said they should have kept their god in their own country. "They believed they were better," he said. He made a little noise in his throat and told the boy that it was dangerous to think this way. He said that too much self-belief could come back to injure you.

"Did she pray?" he asked the boy.

The boy said that he did not understand.

The lieutenant smiled, and he did not stop smiling. He said, "Trust me."

Then he asked if the girl could swim. Because if she couldn't swim, then she must have drowned.

The boy said he didn't know about this, if the girl could swim or not.

The lieutenant ignored the boy. He said that the ocean was dangerous at that place. A week earlier a fisherman had drowned there. He stood and lit another cigarette and closed his eyes and then opened them. Then he sat down at his desk and wrote on the paper and then he looked up and he saw the boy sitting there. He said that he could go.

The boy raised his head and for the first time he looked at the lieutenant's face, which was calm and appeared to hold no malice. The lieutenant repeated again what he had said the first time. "You can go."

The boy stood and dipped his head slightly and he began to back out of the office, but before he reached the door he turned and slipped sideways between the door and the jamb and he went down the hallway, expecting to be called back, or to be caught, but by the time he had reached the main doors which led out onto the street, he knew that, against all odds and contrary to the truth and facts of the case, he was free.

2.

ON THAT DAY, he had been standing in the doorway of a jewellry shop on Quang Trung Street when the girl passed by on her bicycle. He had not seen her since the Sunday when she sat beside him in the small room and he repeated the words that had flowed so easily from her mouth. And then, she had whispered that he was saved. "Oh," she said, "That's wonderful." He had not known, at that moment, what was wonderful, but he was pleased that she was pleased and he had loved the calm of that moment, the stillness, the closed space in which the two of them sat, side by side. At that point he had been carried away and he imagined that it was she who had saved him.

But the stillness had passed and what he experienced in the days that followed was confusion. And shame. Though he did not know it was shame. And so, when the girl passed by on her bicycle he thought of calling out, but he didn't, and instead he took his own bicycle and he followed her. She rode across the bridge and towards the mountain and then up the hill to the trail that led down to Monkey Beach. She locked her bike at the top of the hill and then disappeared. The boy set his bike in a grove of trees and he walked to the edge of the hill and looked down onto the beach. The girl was alone. She wore black shorts and she took these off to reveal a dark blue bathing suit bottom and white legs, and then she removed her top and under that was another part of the bathing suit, and this part covered her breasts. Her stomach was bare. She lay down on her back in the sand and stretched out her arms.

She lay like that and did not move. The boy descended the hill and walked through the sand towards the girl. It was a windy day and the ocean threw itself against the shore. There was a white bird out over the water and it dropped and then rose quickly.

She saw the boy before he spoke. She was surprised and she sat up quickly and covered her chest with an arm and said, "Oh," and then she looked around and back at the boy and asked how he had found her. What was he doing there?

"You rode by," he said. "Very quickly. And I followed you." Then he said it was not safe to be here. It was a lonely beach.

The girl looked about. She said that she had been here before.

The boy nodded and then he said that he wanted to sit beside her. Was that okay?

She shook her head. She wanted to be alone. Then, she reached out and touched his arm and said, "I'm sorry."

On her wrist was a watch with a black strap and this made her skin look very white. The sun was high above them and it was hot and the boy felt the heat against his head. He said that he did not know what was happening. He had done what she wanted. He did not understand her.

The girl said, "No, no. What are you talking about?" Then she laughed, but it was not a happy laugh. She seemed frightened and the boy wanted to tell her that there was no need to be frightened. He was not dangerous.

The girl's arm swung out to take in the sky and the air and the trees behind them and the sand and the sea. When she spoke he did not recognize her voice. It was too high and she spoke too quickly. She said, "All of this. Do you see it? Do you understand that all of this was created by Him?"

The boy said that he understood. "And you," he said. "You too." His hand slid along an imaginary line that ran from her feet to her head. He held his palm near her face and then he touched her jaw and said, "You are very beautiful."

"No," she said and she pushed him away and stood quickly. Brushed sand from the backs of her shoulders. She picked up her bag and her black shorts and shirt and began to walk away. The sun was high in the sky and very bright and very hot and she disappeared into the sun and then reappeared, her hands holding her clothes and her bare back still streaked with sand.

He followed her. He wanted to stop her, to explain that he was a good person, and that his goodness had come from her. He called out and she began to run and so, in order to stop her, he hit her. He picked up a rock the size of a mango and he caught up to her and hit her on the back of the head with the rock.

When she fell, her bag spilled out onto the sand and her right arm twisted upwards behind her back and she lay with one cheek against the sand. He waited for her to stand but she didn't move. He called her name but she just lay there. He heard the sound of the surf and he looked up the hill towards the bicycles and then he looked back down the beach. They were alone. He wondered if the girl was pretending to be hurt, if she was waiting for him to walk away and then she would rise. He knelt and took her hand and said her name again. There was blood on her head and it ran down into the sand. Not much, just a small line of red. Her skin was the colour of the sand and in the glare of the sun it seemed that she and the sand were one and the same.

The boy stood up. He walked away from the girl towards the base of the hill, and then he turned and walked back. There was her purse and beside it was a brush and a tube of lipstick and an unopened letter and some Vietnamese money. The boy picked up these things and put them into the purse and carried them, along with the jeans and shirt, to the spot where the girl had been sitting. Then he went back to the girl. He held her wrist. His own hands were shaking and he could not tell if she was alive. He put his hand up against her mouth in order to feel her breath. He felt nothing. He sat for a long time beside the girl. He did not worry about being seen. He studied the curve of her back to see if it would rise and fall with her breathing. He saw nothing and knew then that the girl was dead. At some point he began to say sorry, and he said this over and over again, as if it were some chant that could raise the girl from the sand. He said it in his own language and he said it in the girl's language. He said it loudly at first and then he only whispered it, until his voice faded away.

Much later, a warm rain began to fall. It started slowly and then grew stronger and came in sideways off the ocean. The boy stood and he took the girl by the wrists and he pulled her towards the water. The rain had soaked the girl and her wet hair covered her face. The boy dragged the body out into the water. He dropped the wrists and pushed the girl out. She floated away and then rolled back. The boy pushed her out farther and attempted to hold her under, but she was stubborn and wouldn't sink. For a long time he stood in water up to his chest and held her down and finally, just as the rain let up, she sank.

The boy walked out of the water, past the girl's bag and shorts and shirt, and on up the hill towards the stand of trees, where he retrieved his bicycle. He climbed on and he rode down towards town. The pavement was slippery from the rain and he rode carefully, aware that if he fell, he would hurt himself.

3.

FOR OVER A YEAR the boy had slept in a small room at the rear of the post office where his uncle, who was not really his uncle, worked as a janitor. He was allowed to be in the room from midnight till 5 a.m., but sometimes his uncle forgot about him and when that happened he slept late and woke hungry. When he went back out onto the streets, he searched for food and money. The Europeans who frequented the restaurant on the harbour would sometimes hand him small amounts of money, but it was not much, and he rarely made enough to buy himself breakfast.

He had worked at a bicycle repair shop, but the pay was meagre and the work was hard and the owner was fond of hitting him with a vice grip, leaving a string of bruises along his thigh. After this, he helped his uncle's wife, pouring petrol into whisky bottles for her to sell to passing motorcyclists. The fumes from the petrol were pleasant, and the wife gave him free cigarettes, but the allure of the tourists and the lives those tourists lived, these were the factors that pulled the boy away from steady work.

One evening, two months before he met Marcie, hungry and in need of money, he dressed up in dark pants and a clean white shirt, borrowed his uncle's shoes that were much too big, oiled his hair, and he walked up to the Pacific Hotel where the German women were known to pick up Vietnamese boys. He stood alongside the brick wall that surrounded the hotel, hands out of his pockets, and by ten o'clock he was in the room of a dark-haired woman who told him, in poor English, that her name was Erika.

"Do you speak German?" she asked.

The boy shook his head.

The woman lit a cigarette and studied him. She waved a pudgy hand and said, "Your shoes."

He was sitting in a chair. His feet did not reach the carpet. He bent forward and slipped out of his shoes. He wasn't wearing socks; his feet were unwashed and showed the shadows of the straps from his flip-flops.

Erika told him to take off his pants and shirt. He did this slowly, his eyes on his own feet. Then he looked up and faced her, his hands covering his genitals.

"Come here," she said and waggled a finger. She was wearing black shoes with high heels and tiny straps.

He stepped forward and turned his head to look at the wall as she took his penis and held it. She put out her cigarette and fondled his testicles until he had an erection.

"Good," she said, and made him lie on his back on the bed.

She undressed and straddled him, took his erect penis and put it inside her. Then she held her big breasts, closed her eyes, and called out, "Bitte, bitte, bitte." After, she handed him whisky in a glass and he pretended to drink while she stroked his chest. When he left, she gave him an equivalent of five dollars in Vietnamese money.

The next night he went back to Erika and they did exactly what they'd done the night before. After, she kissed him on the mouth and said, "Beautiful child. How old are you?"

"Eighteen," he said.

She laughed, poked his chest, and said, "No, no."

She was wearing black panties and her stomach hung over the elastic. Her nipples were almost the size of the small saucers that sat beneath the espresso cups in the café to which the boy went every morning in order to watch the European women with their beautiful shoes.

She took his head and held it between her large hands and pushed a breast against his mouth. "My child," she said.

Then she asked him to walk across the room while she lay on the bed and watched. She told him to bend over and he did so while she inspected his little buttocks and pushed a finger against his asshole. He jumped and she laughed.

On the third and final night another woman was in the room with them. This woman was younger and skinnier. Erika sat on a chair and held herself while the skinny woman climbed onto the boy.

The boy thought that the skinny woman was perfect. She had many rings and bracelets and she wore a very expensive watch that scraped against his shoulder. He was getting used to the sound and smell of love and, after the woman was done, he said, "You are very beautiful."

She laughed and patted his cheek and called him a tiny hairless pig. She said this in German and he did not understand everything, only the word *Schweine*. She then repeated this in English.

He told her the story of his father, who had become very rich raising pigs, but then had died. He said he had no mother. He said that he was hungry.

The beautiful woman laughed and offered him a cigarette and some gum. He took what she offered, and then he left.

4.

HE HAD LOVED her shoes, which were made of soft leather. He liked the flat square toes and the smallness of her feet and he liked it when she wore long pants and the cuffs of the pants folded over the top of the shoes, almost touching the ground, but not quite. She walked long distances in shoes that were not made for walking. Her name was Marcie. She lived with five other foreigners, two Brits and three Americans, in a two-storey house close to the train station. On Sundays she sang songs with her friends and invited whoever was willing to join them. She met the boy on the street and asked him to come and he went once. Crackers and juice were served and cheese as well, but the boy didn't like cheese. It was soft and tasted bitter and it left his mouth dry.

He saw her on the streets. She rode her bicycle around town, her bag in the basket, and when it rained she held her umbrella with one hand. Once, after she got off the ferry that took her across the river, she stopped and bent forward and removed her shoes and socks and continued barefoot towards the beach. At some point she dropped a sock. He picked it up and put it in his pocket.

Every other day she mailed a letter. She climbed the stairs to the post office and sat on a wooden bench along the wall and it was here that she addressed her envelopes, and then she went to the wicket and bought stamps. One afternoon, as she stepped out of the post office, he was there and she looked at him and then over her shoulder and then back at him again and she said she had not seen him for a long time. She said that he should come back to the house on Sunday. In the sunlight her hair was lighter, with streaks of copper. He was aware of her fragrance, and he saw her blue eyes and the roundness of her jaw.

She hugged her bag to her chest, breathed in the morning air, and said that in a month she would be going home. "So, you must come," she said.

He agreed.

On that Sunday she sat beside him in the meeting room while an older man named Brian, who seemed to be the leader, stood and told a story about two brothers, one selfish, one kind. Brian spoke very quickly and the boy did not catch everything, but this was no problem, because the only thing the boy really wanted was to be sitting beside Marcie. After Brian had finished speaking, the group sang a song and the boy was amazed at how clear and strong Marcie's voice was. She sat up straight and took deep breaths and he wanted to be the air that she breathed.

Later, she asked him if he was happy.

He said he was. Very.

She said that she didn't know anything about him.

He said that his father was a physician and his mother a lawyer and he was an only child and in two years he would be ready for university and his parents would send him to Michigan, probably. Or California.

Marcie laughed and said that she had not heard anyone use the word physician in that way.

"What should I say?" the boy asked.

"We would say doctor." Marcie waved a hand and said it didn't matter. It was just odd. But okay. Then her face tightened and her voice lowered and she asked him if he knew Jesus.

The boy loved the softness of her voice and the hair that grew on her arms and the shape of her knuckles. She was slightly overweight. Her chin was double. He said maybe.

She asked him if he wanted to talk about Jesus.

"Yes," he said. "I do."

She took his arm and led him into a small room, away from the larger group, and they sat side by side on the edge of a bed. There were posters of rock singers on the wall and there was a white towel on the back of a chair, and shoes lined up by the closet, and there was a pair of jeans crumpled on the floor.

Marcie crossed her legs and told him that Jesus loved him. "He loves you exactly as you are. With all your mistakes, your sins, your ugly thoughts. And he wants to make you whole." She looked at the boy and asked if he wanted to become a Christian.

He said he did.

She went, "Oh," and she squeezed her hands together and said, "That's wonderful." She asked him to close his eyes and repeat after her.

He closed his eyes and then immediately opened them again and he watched her as she spoke, and he said exactly what she said, "Jesus, I am a sinner but I want you to take away my sin and I want you to make me whole. I want to be loved. I want to be good. Please, Jesus." And when she was done she lifted her head and opened her eyes and she reached out to take one of his hands and she held his hand between her own soft palms and she told him that he was saved.

Leo Fell

THE DAY MARIANNE found out she took a swing at him. He was standing in the kitchen, holding his briefcase, confessing failure in the usual circuitous route, talking about possibilities, about a pot he had invented for mountain climbers, when her fist came at his head and he ducked. He felt shame. Here was his wife, beautiful in a small black dress, her hair done up with silver clips and her earrings dancing like insects, while he, Leo Fisher, ducked the blow he deserved.

"You son of a bitch," she said.

For a time he'd sold real estate and then he invested in a land scheme that fell through and he had to take a loan and when his payments fell short he sold off the last of his savings bonds. That was the day that Marianne, beautiful in her rage, went after him. In the winter that followed he tried to sell homemade tomato juice that cured cancer and in the early spring he drove into Northwestern Ontario where he sold Gore-Tex jackets out of cardboard boxes that had been shipped in from China. In early April, when the ice was breaking up on the lakes, he called home and Marianne told him that she had fallen in love and she was telling him now so that her own life didn't have to be a lie. She said that if they moved on with this, no matter what pain it caused—and she knew there would be pain—it was still better for the boys, especially Eric, who was only six and innocent and could be most damaged by anything resembling anger or rage.

She stopped talking and into that silence Leo fell.

"Is he rich?" he asked, stupidly.

"That's not the point."

"What does he do?"

"He's a doctor."

"He's rich."

"You're missing the point."

"Am I? Why don't you lay it out for me?"

"You're raising your voice."

"Really? Okay, what's the point?"

"I love him."

Leo swallowed. Said, "What's his name?"

"Ivan."

"Oh, my. Does Ivan have a big Russian cock?"

"Stop it, Leo."

"He makes you happy."

"He does," Marianne said, and she seemed apologetic and for this Leo was absurdly grateful. He said that he wouldn't be coming home for a while and that she could tell the boys exactly why. Then he hung up. He was calling from the phone booth at Rushing River Campground. He was alone, the park was closed, and he could hear the rapids in the distance. A bird called overhead. A squirrel talked to him from beside an empty garbage can.

That same day he stopped for lunch in Kenora where he fell to talking to Don, a contractor who needed a carpenter. Leo said he had some experience, he'd roughed a few houses in his time, and so he was hired. He found a room at the Walleye Motel. He pinned photographs of his sons above the bureau mirror, laid out his few clothes in drawers, and placed the book he was reading, *War and Peace*, by his bedside. He made himself coffee and watched a baseball game on TV and thought about Marianne spreading her legs for another man. Later, he found himself drinking in a bar near his motel. He had four beers and ordered another. There was a live band and a group of young women danced, skirts flipping and bare legs flashing. He walked home after midnight and phoned Marianne. Her voice was thin and whispering. "I was sleeping, Leo. The boys are sleeping. Call back in the morning."

"I'm a carpenter now, Marianne. A good chunk of cash in that."

"You're drunk, Leo."

"That may be true, but at least I'm not hurting anyone."

"Good night, Leo," she said, and hung up.

IN THE EVENINGS, after work, Leo ate at the restaurant down the street, the Clio, and he always sat at the same table and was served by Girlie, who gave him free refills and steered him away from the poorer dishes.

"Hamburger steak's not great," she said. "Pepper's better." She had dark hair cut short and she was skinny and at first from the back Leo thought she was a boy until she turned and approached him and spoke and he saw the shape of her jaw and her name tag.

One night, after he was more comfortable with her, he asked, "Who gave you a name like that?"

"My mother."

"Don't get me wrong," Leo said, "It's a great name."

"It's a bold question," Girlie said.

"You've never been asked it before?"

"I have. Too many times. I've considered changing my name to Kathy or Donna."

He couldn't have guessed her age. He asked Shaena, the other waitress, how old Girlie was and Shaena laughed and said, "Too young for you." She walked away and came back later and said, "If you can guess her age you get a free meal."

"On her?"

"That's what she said."

"And what if I'm wrong?"

"You take her bowling."

"Bowling?"

"Yeah, that game where you knock pins down with balls."

Leo took a pencil and wrote 25 on a napkin and handed it to Shaena. She looked at it. She was a big woman and her chest rolled as she laughed. She walked away and Leo waited half an hour. He was certain that he had insulted Girlie. Who came finally, holding a pot of coffee, and sat down across from him.

"Are you a hopeful man or just plain generous?"

"I'm an honest man."

"Whoaa, Girlie," she said, and she looked up at the ceiling and then back at Leo. He looked around the restaurant and thought that his life had suddenly changed and he wasn't sure if that was a good thing.

Girlie said, "Well, Leo Fisher, what night do you want to bowl?"

IN THE EVENINGS Leo read in his room and when he tired of that he walked around the town and down to the wharf and stood and looked out across the water to the houses on the far side where the highway followed the shore and then slipped up through the rock and across the shield towards Winnipeg. He looked at the boats with their bright lights and he smoked and thought about home. He called the boys twice a week.

One time Eric answered. "Hello, Eric speaking,"

Leo said, "Hi, guy, it's me," and Eric took a breath, said, "Hi, Dad," and then asked, "Where are you?"

"Kenora."

"Where's that?"

"Not far. By a lake. Are you being good?"

"Bob died."

"Who's Bob?"

"The fish, Dad. At school. He was orange and black. Ish."

"What happened?"

"He was upside-down this morning. Julie said he was old."

"Julie?"

"Dad." A quick rebuke, then, "My teacher."

"I knew that." Leo heard the boy laugh, a snort. "What'd you eat for supper?"

"Cornflakes."

"Is Mommy there?"

"She's cutting a customer. The hair."

"She is?"

"Hmmm, hmmm."

"Okay, do you love me?"

"Yes."

"I love you too."

"I know." Very certain, his voice strong. "Ivan's here for supper."

"He is?" Leo laughed, as if this were natural and good. He said, "What you having? Sauerkraut?"

"What's that?"

"It's okay, son. I'm sorry. Could you tell your mother to come to the phone?"

Eric disappeared and there was nothing. The occasional cough, a door shutting, Eric talking to someone, a man's low voice—this is what Leo heard. He finally hung up and looked around his room. He lay back on his bed and thought he should make plans to go home to see the boys on the weekend. Or, to bring them up to the lake.

HE WAS TO MEET Girlie in front of the lanes on 3rd Street. Leo got there first. He stood on the sidewalk like a sentinel. When he saw Girlie coming he was both surprised and happy. He had arrived in a strange land and Girlie was it. She was wearing jeans and boots and a black tank top and carrying a black purse over one shoulder. When she saw Leo she lifted a hand as if she were showing him her palm and then she lowered it. She walked up to him and stopped and said, "Hiya, Leo."

"Hello, Girlie. Are you ready?" He bent at his knees, threw one arm forward, one backward, and said, "The bowler."

She led him up the stairs and into the dark of the bowling lanes where they sat and Leo, bending to tie his shoes beside Girlie, smelled a mixture of coconut and apple.

Girlie wanted to bet a dollar on each game and by the end Leo had lost three dollars though he didn't mind because with each strike Girlie did a little dance. After, they went for beer at a bar down the street. It was ten o'clock. Leo asked, "What about your boy?" and Girlie said, "He's with my mother for the night." She had her elbows on the table and her arms were folded.

Leo said, "I've got a boy who's six. Eric. And one more, Scott, who's sixteen." Leo looked at Girlie's face and then at her hands. He folded his own hands, as if praying, and said, "And there's Marianne, I'm married to her. Though she's leaving me for a Russian doctor."

"I'm not stupid," Girlie said. "I talked to Don."

"Well, that's good," Leo said. Then he said it again, "That's good," as if everything were clear and fine and motives were obvious and they were, just the two of them, walking hand-in-hand down a road with their backs to the troubles behind them.

"Don said you were an inventor," Girlie said.

Leo tapped out a cigarette and offered Girlie one. She accepted and he lit a match and reached across and she held his hand and bent her head towards the match. Her fingers dragged across his thumb as she pulled away and exhaled.

"I was," Leo said. "But then I've been many things. Salesman, garbage collector, taxi driver."

"So what have you invented?"

"A pot."

"Yeah?"

"For mountain climbers. It's cone shaped so it uses less fuel and heats water faster." On a napkin he drew the design and labelled it.

"From here it looks like a dunce cap," she said. Then, seeing his face, she took his hand and asked, "And you sold this, this pot?"

"I tried. Nobody wants it."

"That's amazing," Girlie said, "It's like you're a poet or something. You know?"

"That's nice of you to say. Marianne, my wife, sees my inventions as shit."

"Oh, she doesn't."

"Yes, she does."

"Well, I don't," Girlie said, and she raised her glass and drank and Leo saw, through the bottom of the glass, her open mouth, her teeth, the tip of her tongue and later, in bed beside her, he remembered that image and placed his finger gently under her top row of teeth, said, "Bite," and she did.

They had walked, after leaving the bar, up the sidewalk slowly, prolonging the evening. She said, at his motel, "Can I?" looking at the door and back at him.

Perhaps it was loneliness, perhaps need. He did not think, he just said, "Are you sure?"

She said, "I'm thirty-five and you're forty-three and my mother doesn't baby-sit often and I'm not gonna wait till you divorce your wife and besides I've been thinking about this for the last week, so how about it?"

"That's a great speech," Leo said and he took her into his room and made coffee while Girlie explored the bathroom and looked out the patio doors to the alley. She turned and said, "I love hotel rooms. Our family could never afford them."

"This one's a motel and it's cheap," Leo said.

Girlie made a little noise in her throat. She sat on the bed and took off her boots and socks and stood and slipped out of her jeans. She sat again and bounced on the edge of the bed. Her legs were thin and white. Leo watched. The coffee gurgled through the maker. She shrugged off her tank top. She wasn't wearing a bra and her breasts were small and she bounced again and her chest barely moved and she said, "Come on, Leo Fisher. We'll drink coffee after."

Leo went to her. He said, "I've never done this before."

"You want to stop?"

"No."

"Then, can I ask you something?"

"You can." Her hands were locked at his spine. He could feel her ribs with his own hands.

"Could we pray first?"

"How's that?"

A car passed in the alley. The headlights scraped the curtains and then passed on.

"Come," she said and she kneeled by the bed and Leo kneeled beside her and she said, "Dear Jesus, here I am. This is Girlie. I want to thank you for Leo. I'm so happy that he came into my restaurant and sat at a table where I was serving. It's like you reached down your hand and guided Leo my way. Amazing. I want to say thanks for sex, too, for the joy of horniness, for how I feel right now. Wow. Thank you, Jesus. Amen."

Leo was watching Girlie. She was naked except for her panties and he listened to her pray and looked at her thin shoulders and the curve of her spine in the dim light and he thought laughter might be a good remedy here but he didn't laugh because Girlie had opened her eyes and was looking at him.

"You just talk?" he asked.

"I do."

"And someone listens?"

"Of course. Do you want to touch me now?"

He had not held anyone for a long time. With Marianne in the past year there had been very little sex and when there was she masturbated him, lying like a clinician beside him, dreaming, he imagined, of vodka-induced hard-ons, and so, when Girlie slipped a condom on him and put him inside her, he entered a strange and unknown country, a place where Girlie's hands ran rivers along his back and her legs clamped him to the heart of a vast plain. The journey was dark and simply strange and the clouds above were harmless.

After, she got out of bed and went into the bathroom and sat on the toilet and he saw her through the doorway, sitting primly, hands folded in her lap, and as she peed she tilted her head and after, wiped herself delicately, studied the paper, and dropped it in the toilet. She came back to him, hopping once like a child. He covered her with the blanket and she fell asleep, her mouth against his neck. After a bit he rolled sideways and climbed out of bed and sat at the small table, smoking and watching her. Much later he slid in beside her and she reached out a hand and held his hip as he fell asleep. In the morning she was gone.

ON SATURDAY LEO drove to Winnipeg to see Eric and Scott. He took them out to the Dark Zone and then they went for a late breakfast and he sat across from them and told them about the house he was building, that it had six bathrooms and an indoor pool and an outdoor pool, a Jacuzzi and two kitchens. Leo drew a picture of the house and walked Eric through it.

Scott huddled against the window and watched the street. Leo asked him how school was.

"It's okay."

"I always hated school," Leo said.

Eric watched him, wide-eyed, his mouth full of pancakes.

"Oh, not like that, Eric. I was just kind of a sad student. Not very good at it." He poured cream into his coffee. Said, "So, everybody getting along okay at home?"

Scott looked at him, and then away.

Eric said, "Ivan has a dog. A bit pull."

"Is that right? This dog's living at the house?"

Eric nodded gravely. "In the basement at night. He barks and barks."

"How 'bout you, Scott?" Leo asked, looking for an entry into this boy, but thinking about a big ugly dog messing up the basement he'd renovated.

Scott looked him in the eye. "Ivan's a prick," he said.

"Huh," Leo went, pleased, thinking that his eldest son was an astute evaluator of people.

Eric began to cry.

"What, what?" Leo said. He looked at Scott, who shrugged and said that Eric cried a lot these days. For no reason. Watching TV, eating dinner, he just started to cry.

Leo wiped Eric's eyes and nose. He kissed his head. On the way back home he said that he would take the boys up to Kenora and they'd go fishing. "In an eighteen-foot aluminum boat we'll wind our way through the Lake of the Woods," he said.

Neither of the boys answered.

At the house, Marianne was working in the flowerbed along the sidewalk. She was wearing shorts and an old T-shirt and when she saw him she waved and came towards him. She leaned into the window. Her mouth had always been a little crooked so that it appeared as a sneer and today the sneer was more pronounced. Leo said, "God, you're beautiful."

"Surprise, surprise."

"I was thinking that we should try to work things out. That the boys would be happier with me than a guy called Ivan."

Marianne shook her head. "You always try to be funny, Leo. Especially when something bad has happened. Besides, there's a lot of things that would have to change."

"Make me a list. I'll start on it today."

"Don't do this, Leo. You're just killing yourself."

Leo tapped the chrome on the window of his Riviera and looked out at Eric, who was sitting on the front step, waiting.

"Eric started crying," he said.

Marianne's voice went soft. "I know. The psychologist says he's figuring things out."

"The psychologist? You're sending him to a fucking psychologist? Jesus Christ, Marianne. Who do you think we are?" He lifted a hand and went ahhh and then he said, "Ivan's paying for it. Isn't he?"

"Actually, yes. And I think it's quite wonderful."

"Wonderful?" Leo said. He blew up his cheeks and exhaled and then honked his horn and called out the passenger window, "Hey, Eric, give your Dad a wave."

Eric lifted a hand. Moved his fingers slightly. "Love you," Leo called. He turned to Marianne and said, just before he backed out of the driveway, "Get the fucking pit bull out of my basement."

For the first half hour, just before he slipped the Buick into cruise control, he was quite happy, very pleased to have gotten in the last word, to have made a statement about his rights, to have sent a minor message to Marianne. But then, near the Steinbach turnoff, he felt a heaviness enter his chest and by the time he passed Richer he was disgusted with his actions and his anger and he thought he should call Marianne and apologize. But, he didn't.

When he got back to Kenora, he walked over to Canadian Tire and bought himself a pair of workboots and on the way home he passed a bar, so he went inside. He sat by himself and drank and watched the strippers and thought that everybody wanted something and then there were those few who wanted everything. Several times that evening he told himself to go home but then another drink appeared and the time passed and tomorrow seemed far away. Around midnight a man with a ponytail and a wide forehead sat at the table next to Leo and asked for a cigarette. Leo held out the pack. The man took a cigarette and lit up. He looked at Leo and said, "Four years ago there was this man, Leonard Minaruk, who went out in his boat. Out into the lake among the islands and he got lost. Never came back. Last year a fisherman found his skeleton hanging from a tree. People figured Leonard was lost and what with winter coming on he was about to starve to death and instead of dying slowly he hung himself with the lead from the boat."

Leo was watching the man. He waited for more but the man had stopped talking. Leo cleared his throat. "That it?"

"Pretty much." The man shrugged. Took another cigarette and then stood, shook hands with Leo and said, "Nice meeting you."

"Same," Leo said.

"Do you need help?" the man said. "You're drunk."

"I'm walking," Leo said.

"Walking's good," the man said. "It clears the head." And he disappeared.

Half an hour later, Leo left the bar. He stood on the sidewalk for a long time and looked left and then right. He looked straight ahead and went over to the curb and sat between two parked cars. Time passed. He lay back against the concrete and watched the sky. He fell asleep and was woken by the man he'd met in the bar. He was standing over Leo, telling him to move or he would drive over his legs. Leo lifted his head and looked down at his feet on which there was a pair of workboots that he did not recognize. He called out to the man above him, "It's okay, those aren't my feet."

IN THE MORNING he woke in his own bed and he lay there trying to recall how he had come to this place, but he could not remember. He arrived at work in the afternoon. Ron did not ask where he had been, just sent him up to the roof. He worked well through the early afternoon and then, just after coffee break, he fell. He was up on the trusses, near the peak, nailing in the ridge pieces. He ran out of spikes and was going back to the ladder, using the trusses as stepping stones when his foot slipped and he fell between the twenty-two-inch space of the rafters. He managed to hold on to a truss long enough to rip the palm of his hand open and then continued his fall to the second floor, landing on the hammer that had stayed in his apron. He tried to get up but fell back and looked up at the sky beyond the rafters. He swore. Ron appeared.

Leo looked at him and said weakly, "I'm a bird."

Ron and Jem helped Leo down the ladder, one on either end. Ron put him in his pickup and drove him to the hospital where X-rays showed no bones broken, only a bruised hip. Leo went back to his motel room, swallowed some Tylenol 3, and climbed into bed and slept till it was dark. He woke, in pain and disoriented. He focused on the window, heard the traffic pass, and remembered where he was.

Girlie called.

"Ron told me," she said.

"Don't come over," Leo said, "I'm useless like this."

"I could rub lineament on you. Feed you."

"I'm fine," Leo said.

She came anyway. She brought soup in a Thermos and egg salad sandwiches and coffee. He ate sitting up in bed while Girlie held his knee through the cover of sheets. She said, "I'll do your laundry." She gathered his dirty clothes and put them in a bag. Carried them out to her car and disappeared. When she came back his dirty dishes were lined up under his bed. He'd crawled to the bathroom, brushed his teeth, and crawled back. She bent to kiss him and he smelled the outside air on her, summer, things green.

At night he woke and stood by the window and looked out at the night. A vehicle passed down the alley and he saw within the car the shapes of two people, one large, one small. He thought of Eric and Scott and saw that no amount of back-pedalling could change who he was as a father. He went back to bed but did not sleep until dawn and when he woke again it was noon and a jar of flowers sat on the bedside table.

On the third day after his fall, he rose and showered, dressed and walked down to the docks and sat and watched the gulls. He drank coffee and then walked back to his room where he found his door open. Fletcher and Girlie were sitting on the bed, his freshly folded laundry between them. The sight of the laundry depressed Leo. He hobbled over to the chair.

"Look at you," Girlie said. She stood and took his hand, as if shyness were something she'd just learned, and she looked up at him and smiled stupidly.

"Happy, happy," Leo said. He sat down. "Hiya, Fletcher," he said.

Fletcher rolled onto his back and held his hands over his eyes.

Girlie sat down beside Leo. Held his arm. He could smell her and he imagined little squirts of cheap perfume landing on her body, up her legs, between her breasts.

She bit his neck.

"I'm hungry," he said.

So the three of them walked up to Boston Pizza, the place through which Leo had first entered the town, and they sat and drank beer and ate garlic toast and watched a tennis match on TV while Fletcher drew on the placemats. Girlie took Leo's hand and said, "What is it?"

"Nothing."

"Nothing?" Girlie cast her eyes about. Said, "I was thinking about you. I'm very happy you know."

"I can see that." Leo studied her hands, the veins in her forearms, her chapped elbows. Fletcher had slipped off the chair and was sitting under the table. Leo said, "I've been thinking about my boys. I've got two hands and they're both full and I just don't know how to pick up or even hold onto someone else."

Girlie blinked. "You talking 'bout Fletcher? This is what you've been worrying about?"

"Sometimes."

"Fletcher'll be fine. Children can wade through almost anything."

Leo shook his head. "No, they can't."

And then he went, "Ahh, never mind. It's probably my fall. I feel like a boat out on a sea, and holes get punched in the sides, and then it sinks."

"I could pray for you. Would you like that?"

"Prayer doesn't work."

"Oh, it does, Leo. If you try. It won't give you things or fill your pockets but it feels good."

Her belief was infectious, but it left him sad. She said good-bye to him at his motel door, kissed him on the mouth and walked away, holding Fletcher's hand, her shoes clacking out a code and then fading.

During the night he woke from a dream in which he fell again and again from a high place. He held off sleep for a long time, afraid to return to that dream. He turned on the bedside lamp and his arm appeared, a stick that belonged elsewhere. It was grotesque, too thin, the bump at the wrist seemed to grow. He drew the arm close and smelled it, discovering his own scent.

In the morning he phoned home. The phone rang and rang and he let it ring, thinking how he would tell Marianne that he had fallen off a roof, just slipped between the rafters, and dropped like a rock. But then he'd bounced back and he was okay.

He waited for Marianne to pick up. Or someone.

Man Lost

THE BOY WAS six when his father first took him out beyond the lip of the reef to fish. They left at dawn and returned at dusk with red and black snappers and five good-sized tuna and a barracuda bigger than the boy himself. The snappers were pulled from the deep deep, sometimes three on one line, with bulging eyes and stomachs stuck in their mouths. The barracuda put up a fight and for a time the boy had held the rod, his father's arms around him, and the boy could feel the strength and the power and the wildness, though at that age he would not have known that particular word, and it was his father who called out, as the fish drew near to the boat, "Lookit the wildness." And his father had bent to retrieve the grappling hook and speared the barracuda, and still it fought. And then his father picked up a small wooden baseball bat, and he clubbed the barracuda over the head, once, twice, three times, until the big fish stopped moving. "Here," his father said, "You have a go," and he handed the bat to the boy and the boy took it and leaned over the gunnel and hit the fish on the head, once, and then again. The fish was already dead.

His father pulled the barracuda over the gunnel into the bottom of the boat. He took his knife and his whetstone and he sharpened the knife and he replaced the whetstone and then he removed the dorsal and pectoral fins with a clean stroke, and then cut the fish open, from the tail fin up to the head, along the belly. He found the liver and cut off a small piece and placed it under his tongue and waited ten seconds and then he spit the piece of liver into the water and he said, "She's safe."

The boy watched his father clean the fish, and rub the scales off with the sharp end of the knife, and he watched his father clean his hands and knife in the water of the ocean. His father cleaned his hands and knife often, as if this were the most important thing, and the boy watched his father throw the insides of the fish overboard and he watched the pink offal turn to grey and to black as it sank. He watched as his father cut off the head and stored it at his feet. His father said, "For the soup." The boy didn't ask questions, for his father did a lot of talking as he worked, naming and explaining, and so it was that the boy began to learn the skills that would take him into his teens and to the age of twenty-two when, just married, he would buy his own boat and fit it with a used two-stroke sixty horse Evinrude, and so equipped, he would leave his wife in bed at 5 a.m. and head out to the edge of the reef to catch snapper and tuna and return at dusk to sell the fish by the pound to the local restaurants where tourists came to eat.

His name was Quinn, and when he fished, he fished alone, save for the days when tourists hired him and then he asked his father to come along, simply because tourists were a lot of work, and there were too many lines to keep track of. The pay was good. Better than fishing for oneself. And usually the tourists didn't want the fish, just a photo of themselves holding up the biggest fish, something to talk about. And so, on those days when he worked for the tourists, he could depend on cash and he could count on fish to sell, and on those days he was pleased and his wife, Faustina, was pleased and they fell asleep late at night, their boy between them, talking about their plans for maybe a second boat and hiring Quinn's brother, who worked as a captain on the diving boat at Chillies, and eventually, a fleet of boats, with Quinn as owner and manager and Faustina as accountant. They would find a bigger house, and furnish it with beds and tables and chairs built by Isak, the carpenter two doors down, a man whose skill as a woodworker was renowned on the island. And so it was that they dreamed.

He sold his catch, mostly snappers and tuna, by the pound to Greens, and with these earnings he bought fuel, lines, and bait and he gave the remaining cash to Faustina, who put it in a tin box and slid it under the bed. Faustina was a woman who believed that most folks thought and acted the way she did, that everyone had her values, the same big heart, the trenchant faith, the easygoing love for humanity. Even when she was proved wrong, she would shake her head and say that this person or that person, those that had committed some errant evil, only needed to be rehabilitated and all would be fine. Rehabilitation was always on Faustina's mind. She went to church three times a week, and she attended prayer meeting with the women on Wednesdays and she made cakes for the children with AIDS at the local hospice. She loved Quinn. She loved their son. He was one, but he already resembled his father. Burly, broad across the shoulders, easy to grin, gentle. Every morning at four, Faustina rose with Quinn and boiled him coffee and fixed him a sandwich and sent him off with a palm against his back, a slight pressure, the imprint of which he felt throughout the day.

Quinn wore a long-sleeved black T-shirt, and he covered his face, up to his eyes, with a second T-shirt, his son's, that he pulled up from his neck to cover his nose, and so, plying the waters off the coast of the islands, he resembled a man who did not want to be identified.

IT WAS DURING the high season, in early January, that K. appeared. He had on his arm a dark-haired white-skinned woman, very thin with large breasts and he introduced her as Yvonne and he said that they wanted to go fishing and so he hired Quinn for two days. K. was voluble and within the first hour of the first day Quinn knew much about his life. He was an owner of five car dealerships in Dallas, one of them Audi, and he had a girlfriend back home, and he had an ex-wife and twins, and Yvonne was from Detroit and they'd met the night before and she'd insisted that she wanted to go deep sea fishing. "Here we are," he said, and he laughed in a manner that was forced, a laugh that Quinn would come to recognize over the next two days, and the year following when K. would return for another round, as a command to join in.

On this day Quinn had asked his father for help, and so it was that his father sat in the bow with Yvonne and flirted with her and told her stories about working the cruise ships as a younger man and the women that fell over him, and about fishing as a young boy and about his children, of which he had six, though one, a daughter, had died of AIDS and another, a son, had died in prison in Tegucigalpa. All stories that Quinn had suffered the telling of again and again. Yvonne seemed taken with the older man, with the calluses on his hands and his sincere tone and the attention he paid her. Late afternoon, after dropping the couple off on shore, Quinn's father announced that Yvonne's beauty had been hard earned. "Her breasts weren't real," he said.

The following morning Quinn and K. went out alone. K. wore a purple bandana and silver sunglasses and he went shirtless. He had tufts of hair around his nipples, otherwise his chest was like a child's. He said that he wanted to do some serious fishing. He wanted to catch a big fucking fish. A marlin.

Quinn said that open water was where the big marlin were and that the wind was too high and the waves unpredictable.

K. said that he wasn't afraid of waves or wind.

Quinn said that they'd have to plan in advance. "We'd need more drinking water, and we'd need lunch, and we'd need a jerry can of gas, and we'd have to tell someone that we were going out. Another time." He said that the cost would be double.

"Triple'd be fine," K. said. "Long as we catch a big one." He was quiet as Quinn set the lines.

At noon K. pulled in a small tuna and Quinn cut it up for bait. At the western tip of the island he reset the lines and turned back into the wind. And that's when K., who had been sullen and silent up till then, began to enliven. He said that the night before he'd met the most beautiful woman in the world. "God, she was gorgeous," he said. He made no mention of Yvonne, and Quinn didn't ask. "Beautiful girl," K. said. He said that finding a woman was as easy as selling a car. He snapped his fingers and said that ever since he was a teenager

he'd known the language of selling. "Folks are easily convinced. Confidence is all. Tell them a story, flatter them, keep
talking, talk some more, that's the trick. Diversion's necessary.
Don't allow them time to think. Thinking gets everyone in
trouble. This girl for example, she was alone at the bar and I'd
noticed her and when she went to the washroom I caught her
eye and on her way back to her seat I halted her, touched her
arm, and said that she was the most beautiful woman I'd ever
seen. I didn't let her answer, I just kept talking. Said my name,
what I did, that I was a businessman who sold Audis and that
I'd love to buy her a drink and when she said that she'd rather
I buy her an Audi I knew I had her. We sat at the bar. She was
a local girl. Twenty-two. When I heard this, I dropped my age
some. She asked if I was married and I said not anymore. She
asked if I had children and I said none. Which is true, but
that's another story. I asked her if she was single, and she said
she could be if it was necessary. And that's the moment when
you know that the fish is on the line and she'll be easy to pull
in. You married?" he asked.

Quinn nodded.

"Children?"

"One."

"Boy or girl?"

"Boy."

"Sweet. How old?"

"One."

"Your wife's name?"

"Faustina."

He repeated it. Then asked, "She from here?"

"She is."

"You don't have much, do you Mr. Quinn?"

"What do you mean?"

"This boat, for example, is it yours?"

"It is."

"You have a house?"

"I rent."

"A car? Motorcycle?"

"No. None of those."

"But you're happy."

"What do you mean?"

"You're satisfied. When you go home to your boy and your wife in the evening you think to yourself, This is a good life."

"I have a good life."

"You see? Why do you think that is?"

"I don't know."

"You have only a boat and a wife and a son and some fish to put on your table and this is enough."

"Is there more?"

"Fuck yeah." He reached into his pocket and pulled out a money clip with folded bills, denominations of one hundred. About twenty of them. "This," he said. "And getting laid by a beautiful woman. And driving an Audi R8. But the money in my pocket, that gives me a hard-on. You know what I mean to say?"

"Money is your pill."

"Ha. Yes. Exactly. What's yours?"

Quinn said that he was satisfied.

"You'd have loved this girl last night." He studied Quinn. Asked, "You lift weights?"

"I do."

"I can see that. Built like a fullback. You play football?"

"American football? Or soccer?"

"American."

"No."

"You could."

K. stopped talking, and for this Quinn was grateful. He thought that there was no purity like the purity of a fish that has taken a hook and will fight and fight. And then die. But even in death it was pure. He loved fish. Admired their pride and their simplicity. He would take a fish for company any time over a man like this car dealer. Except that the car dealer paid more money. And money was a necessity.

He dropped K. off at dusk at West Bay. They shook hands and K. handed him five hundred dollars. Quinn thanked him.

"I'll return," K. said. "And when I do we'll go out into the deep sea and we'll catch a big one."

"That would be good," Quinn said, and he pocketed the money.

TWO MONTHS LATER, when Quinn's sister Clarita came to visit Quinn and Faustina, she told them that she was pregnant. She was distraught, for she had a job to keep at the Coffee Bean, steady work that paid well, and she had no prospects for taking care of the child and she didn't know if she should keep it.

"You'll keep it," Faustina said. "Something will work out. What about the father?"

Clarita didn't answer at first. Then she said that the father didn't know about it. "He's from away," she said.

"Oh, Clarita," Faustina said. "Shouldn't you tell him?"

"It wasn't even sex. Not really. It was late, and I'd been drinking, and he cornered me, and something happened, though I didn't know what happened till later. I thought we were just fooling around."

Faustina was holding her little boy. She handed him to her husband, who was listening and was aware of a blossoming in his chest and his head.

"He raped you?" Faustina asked.

"No. At least I don't think so."

"Well, girl, either you chose him or you didn't. Did you?"

"I don't know."

"What was his name?" Quinn asked, his voice low and quiet.

Clarita shook her head. "It doesn't matter."

"Did he sell cars?" Quinn asked.

Clarita looked up quickly at her brother and then looked away. She wore her hair very short and she liked very short skirts and short tops and everything else about her was tall and thin, almost stretched out. She tugged at her short skirt now, as if attempting to hide her legs. She said that he sold cars, yes.

"Audis?"

"Yes." She looked at her brother and this time she didn't look away. "Do you know him?"

"I know him. But not like you know him."

WHEN THE BABY was born, Quinn said that the child's name would be Moses, because he was like an infant that had been put in a pitch basket and sent down the river to be found by slaves washing clothes on the bank of that river. He was not a religious man, but his wife Faustina was, and Clarita was as well, and he knew they would like the name, and the reason for the name. Quinn and Faustina took the child in and raised it. Clarita came by for visits once a week, but she had little attachment to the child. Faustina, on the other hand, loved the child as much as she loved her own, who took a proprietary approach to the infant that had landed in bed beside him. They slept with their hands interlocked, or feet touching. The two were as one.

Quinn had been reticent to take in a child that was not his, but he was quickly smitten by the baby's nature, his lack of crying, his delight in shiny objects and his attention to the sound of the wind blowing through the house. Quinn began to carry Moses around in the evening, jostling him in one arm, while his own child demanded the other arm.

"Like two footballs," Quinn said, and he grinned at his wife.

Eventually, within six months, the baby was seen as Quinn and Faustina's child. Some in the community were even convinced that they had seen Faustina walking around in the months previous, heavy with the child that would come to be known as Moses. The family did nothing to dissuade others from this belief.

A year passed. Moses learned to walk. He grew strong. His legs filled out. He didn't have Quinn's son's heft or height, but he had a certain swagger, and there were times, when Quinn came upon him by surprise, that Quinn was struck by the child's eyes, and his mouth, and he saw, ever so briefly, a man with a money clip and barbarous privilege. But it was too simple to equate the child with the father, and so he taught the boy to move softly through the world and he modelled the art of waiting, which was something he had learned long before as a young boy while fishing with his father, and then honed to a fine skill as a young man in his own boat. Patience presided over and usurped the sins of the world, though Quinn did not hold to any notion of sin or wrongdoing. Consequence was all.

AND THEN, WITH the inevitability of the seasons, during the rains this time, K. reappeared. Quinn had heard from his brother that he was being sought by a brash man with skinny legs, and he knew from the description who the man seeking him was, and he avoided being found until one evening, at dusk, washing out his boat after a day of fishing, he heard his name being called and when he rose from the bottom of the boat he saw K. standing in the gloom, grinning, and he thought, Here we go.

He flaunted a paunch, and his legs were white sticks, and he wore a T-shirt that said Filthy, Stinking, Rich: Two Out of Three Ain't Bad. Quinn thought everything cruel that could be thought. He regretted ever knowing this man.

He waited. Did not speak.

"I'm back," K. cried.

Quinn nodded.

"Ready for the big one?"

Quinn bent to wipe the last of the bow. He rose. Shouldered his gear and moved on.

K. followed. "Hey, how about tomorrow. We go out into the deep."

"The water's rough," Quinn said. He had stopped walking for he had no desire to lead this man back to his house. He looked down upon that distended paunch. Here was an ugly man.

"I've got three days. And then I go home. I've been scouring the island for you."

"Why me? There are lots of other outfits."

"They won't go out where I want to go."

"They're smart."

"And you?"

"I'm smart too. I won't do it. Storm season."

"A thousand dollars."

"Not enough."

"Two."

"Thousand."

"Yes."

"No guarantees we'll get something. Oh, we'll get something, but not necessarily what you wish for. Two days. A thousand a day. And you'll pay up front."

"Absolutely." He was full of glee. He reached into his pocket and pulled out the money clip and counted out the bills. He handed them to Quinn, who slipped them into his pocket, and motioned at the shore. "Tomorrow at five a.m. then. Bring a slicker. It'll be raining."

K. wanted to shake hands. Quinn acquiesced. They said goodbye and Quinn climbed the quiet street to his home.

When he told Faustina, she said that the man was dangerous. And evil. And they didn't need the money. "He'll take Moses if he knows," she said.

"He doesn't know, and he won't know, and even if he did know he wouldn't know what to do with that knowledge," Quinn said. They were lying in bed. The boys slept in the bed abutting theirs. The boys were naked. Their legs were entwined. Faustina stroked Moses's head.

"Sometimes I feel guilt," she said. "Like I'm hiding and it's just a matter of time."

He took her hand and kissed it. Pushed his face against her thick hair and breathed in. He rolled her body onto his. Wrapped his arms around her. He was big, she was small. His heart opened. He loved her with great madness.

THEY WERE TO meet in the morning by the beach where the abandoned sailboat was moored in open water, the boat off of which the kids swung out over and tumbled into the clear water at the edge of the coral. At five he was waiting. At five thirty K. arrived. K. wore shorts and a T-shirt, no hat, no slicker. They climbed in and Quinn pushed off and clambered aboard and started the motor. The water beyond the bay was rough and the wind came from the southwest and it was strong and the swells were deep. In the trough there was only water to be seen and at the crest there was the shape of the tip of the island and a brume that floated over the trees. There were no other boats on the water. They ploughed out to sea and within an hour K. was throwing up, his head hanging over the gunnel. "You want me to turn around?" Quinn asked.

"Not on your life," K. said. He was hung over and his eyes looked dead. He grinned.

Quinn held the throttle in the crotch of his elbow and set a chugger and let the line float out and it caught the current and spooled out a thousand feet and then he set the handle in the plastic holder and the boat rolled on the surf and they waited and watched and K. threw up one last time and he washed his face with salt water and he came up grinning and said, "I'm empty."

By noon they'd caught a few small tuna. Not to K.'s liking. Early afternoon, the sea swelled and turned black and the small motor whined as the boat climbed and then sputtered as they fell along the walls of the swells. They took water. Quinn told K. to bail. He did so, his face white. Quinn pulled in the lines. He turned the skiff with some difficulty and pointed them back to the islands.

"Can you swim?" Quinn asked.

"I can float," K. said. He found his phone and took a picture of the ocean.

When the engine died it was near dusk and immediately the wind was pushing them north, parallel to the coast of the mainland. Quinn pulled the cover off the Evinrude and cleaned the plugs and replaced them. He held a thumb to one of the plugs and pulled the starter. A shock went through his thumb. He ate a sandwich that Faustina had prepared. Offered one to K. but he refused, horrified by Quinn's nonchalance.

With darkness the winds shut off and it was absolutely calm, silent save for the slap of the boat on the water.

"What now?" K. asked.

"We wait for morning."

"You've done this before."

Quinn laughed.

At night the sky was clear and the stars were myriad and the moon lit up the water and there were fish jumping and Quinn thought that there were much worse ways to spend a night. The smell of the boat, the salt, the fish at his feet, the gasoline leaking uselessly, the brine on his hands, the scent of his son on the shirt covering his nose. He slept and woke to see K. teetering at the gunnel, pissing into the ocean. Leaning back to look at the sky.

K. zipped and sat and looked at Quinn and said that he'd been married three times. All unlucky. The third marriage was the direst. He said 'direst' with a twist to the word, as if he'd just discovered it and the failed marriage along with it. And he talked, as if to stay the morning and the empty ocean. "Donna was pregnant with twins and I was ecstatic because I'd always wanted kids. They're the one thing money won't buy if you catch my meaning. And so the twins are born, boy girl, and the girl comes first and so she's the eldest right and sometimes at night I enter their room and watch them sleeping in separate cribs, on their backs, their arms thrown upwards in surrender and I think that there is nothing sweeter than a sleeping child. My children. And they grow and grow and one day when they're three, my daughter, who's a terrific talker already, says a name, Sebastian, and I ask who's Sebastian and she says Mommy's friend and he takes us to the playground, and I want to know more of course, because I'm a glutton for pain, and so I ask her simple questions like how often do they go and what kind of car does Sebastian drive and then I ask if Sebastian and mommy hold hands and she says always and my heart just falls because I've known something is amiss, not right in the household of K., but I keep this information in my head, keep it there tight and safe and I harbour it and of course it poisons me. I start looking at the twins, their teeth, their noses, their hair, the colour of their eyes, if they're bowlegged like me, and I notice differences between me and them and I start to think that maybe there is nothing of me that resides in them, you know, not one bit of DNA or genetic material. Some days I am so certain it breaks my heart, and on other days I say you are a fool K. What's to worry? But I have to know, of course, I am one for knowing, and so I order a kit online and one night I creep into the bedroom and swab the twins' mouths and I place the swabs in prepared envelopes and send it away for testing and six weeks later a letter comes for me in the mail, at my office, and I open the envelope, my hands shaking, and I learn the truth."

K. stopped talking. He said that he was thirsty. Quinn handed him the water bottle and advised him to only take a sip. "All we have left," he said.

K. grunted and drank and stoppered the bottle and handed it back to Quinn.

"Of course I want to kill Donna. But I don't. One evening after the twins are in bed I pour a scotch and sit across from her where she's watching Netflix and I shut her laptop and say that I know. She plays innocent at first, and then after much denial and eventual weeping, it comes out. I call her all sorts of names, they just spill out of me, and even as I'm saying all these awful things to her I'm thinking that this is safer than strangling her, or myself, for that is what I am capable of, hurting her or myself. Donna imagined that she would keep the children to herself, and for a time I fight this, but then I become heavy footed and heavy hearted and I stop seeing the kids, which is a form of punishment to myself. And to my kids, who have no concept yet of paternity. Why should they?"

Silence. Quinn was aware of the first tinge of pink to the east. He looked at his watch. He waited.

"Is fucked up," K. said. Then he said, "What's gonna happen?"

Quinn tried to connect K.'s dots. Finally he said, "We wait."

"Maybe a cruise ship will find us and we can cavort."

"Cruise ships hug the coastline. We're in open water."

"Something then. A container ship. A fishing vessel."

"Maybe," Quinn said.

"How long can we last?"

"Three, four days. We don't have much for water."

"And then we die? Like marooned pricks?"

"We won't die."

"Funny. You were sleeping before and I watched you and I thought I could kill you. Easy. Or you me."

Quinn was hunkered by the engine. The night was cool. He had nothing to say.

"I saw your sister. The other day," K. said.

"You know that then. That Clarita is my sister."

"She told me so. She's still a beauty."

They were quiet.

"As the captain of this ship, will you keep me safe?" K. asked.

"Is there danger?"

"Fuck yeah. We're stranded at sea. Lost."

"Not lost," Quinn said. "We'll find the way."

"I'm hungry," K. said.

Quinn plucked a dead tuna from the belly of the boat and he took his knife and he sliced a fillet for K. and handed it to him and said, "Here."

K. took the tuna and ripped off a chunk with his teeth and he chewed slowly, savouring it.

"This will make a good story someday," K. said. "For the twins." He studied Quinn through swollen eyes. "How is your boy?" he asked.

"He is good. Healthy."

"And you have another. Moses."

Quinn said nothing. Felt anger bloom in his head, or maybe it was despair.

K. slept. Quinn kept watch. Slept some and woke with a start. The sun was high in the sky. The water was calm. Utterly still. He took the bottle of water and opened it and wet his mouth. Swallowed. He prodded K. and woke him and handed him the bottle. "Just a little," he said. K. took the bottle and drank deeply. "Enough," Quinn said. He wrenched the bottle from him. A third remained.

K. panted in the bottom of the boat. His lips were dry. His ankles were burned. He looked a scarecrow splayed against the gunnel.

The boat was outfitted with a tattered canvas top and this thin sheet offered some shade if they moved from side to side as the sun climbed. K. spent the day hugging the shadow, speaking little, moaning occasionally. Quinn surveyed the horizon and tinkered with the engine. He pulled it apart and cleaned the carburetor. Put everything back together and pulled the cord. Nothing. He removed the gas line and took in a great quantity of air and held his mouth to the rubber and blew out the line. Bits of dirt, some sand, the remaining petroil. He reset the fuel line and worked the pull. There was a spark and the motor ran for a second and then quit. He spent the remaining daylight dissembling and cleaning the carburetor once again. He cleaned the plugs. Reassembled everything. K. watched.

"Will they be looking for us?"

"Yes," Quinn said. "There will be a search. There will be boats, and there will be planes."

"We are worth it then," K. said, and he smiled.

"They will send out planes because of you. You are worth it."

K. accepted this. The facts were logical.

Even so, an hour later he asked, "Should we start to pray?"

"If you think it'll work."

"My first wife prayed. And prayed. A lost shoe found was an answer to prayer. Your wife, she prays?"

"She does," Quinn said.

"She's certainly praying for you right now."

"Yes."

"Does that give you comfort?"

"I'll take the comfort of my wife's prayers."

"And your boys, they will learn to pray?"

"I imagine. They spend most of their time with their mother."

"Ah, yes, mothers. God bless 'em. Some of them. I heard that four out of ten children born are not sired by the man that thinks he is the father. Those are some numbers. I'd like to meet this Moses. He's a good boy?"

"He is."

"And handsome?"

Quinn nodded.

"Walking?"

"Was at nine months."

"I said to Clarita that if she'd marry me I'd move to the Islands. She said that island life was slow and sleepy. She said that I would find it difficult."

"She's fickle," Quinn said. "And a talker."

"She is," K. said. "And she doesn't keep secrets."

K., as he spoke, was pointing at the sky and following with one eye the line of sight along his forearm. Shearwaters at sea.

At night dolphins swam alongside the skiff. Quinn heard them calling at first and then jumping and when he sat up he saw their shadows slipping through the water. K. had become delirious and was babbling. Quinn, knowing what K. knew, considered various scenarios. Letting the man die at sea from thirst and exposure. Throwing him overboard and watching him paddle about in the tub until he drowned. Saving him and returning to the islands where he could make his claim if he so pleased. It would break Faustina's heart. The rules in Quinn's own heart were conflicted and many. His loyalty was to Faustina and to the boys. And then to Clarita, weak as she was. And then it was to himself and then to his boat and finally to K., a dissolute and feeble man, even though he imagined himself to be strong. This was self-deception at its greatest.

The sun rose in the morning as decreed, crossed the sky, and descended into the far end of the ocean. Disappeared. The water bottle was empty. Quinn caught a blue runner of a medium size and cut fillets and told K. to suck slowly at the meat. He himself held the fillet in his teeth and breathed in and out slowly. Took in the moisture. K. ate quickly and immediately threw up the fish and whatever liquid was left in his body. He moaned. Lay on his side in the bow.

Their third night on the ocean, K. attempted to throw himself into the water. Quinn caught him and tied him with fishing line to the bench at the bow. The salesman thrashed and howled and cursed. Tried to bite Quinn.

The following day, K. was silent, a prostrate and bound form slowly drying out. Quinn again pulled the carburetor and tore it down to its core and laid out the parts on the stern bench upon which he'd placed his son's T-shirt. He had an old toothbrush and with this he cleaned and scrubbed the parts. The sun heated his back. As he inspected the brass fuel jet and the fuel bowl, Quinn found that the tiny hole in the jet was plugged. With a copper wire retrieved from his toolbox he cleaned the hole. He poured a few tablespoons of petroil into the plastic bailer and laid the fuel jet and bowl in the liquid. Lifted the pieces into the air and blew on them. When they were dry, he reinstalled the carburetor. Darkness had fallen by the time the engine was reassembled. K. was silent in the bow. Quinn checked on him and found a pulse. Clouds covered the sky and a light wind had picked up and was pushing them southwest towards Belize. He would wait till morning, when he could gain his bearings, and if the engine fired and started, then he could ascertain his position and point the boat in the right direction. He slept. Woke to check on K., whose breathing was short and bubbly. He slept some more, aware of the wind on his face and the rocking of the boat on the waves, which had grown larger.

In the morning, K. was dead. He knew immediately when he opened his eyes and looked at the body lying in the bow. There was no movement, no breath. A dead man was like a dead fish. No evidence was needed.

He cut off a section of tattered tarp and laid it over K.'s body. He surveyed the sky and noted the direction of the sun as it leaked through the light clouds. His phone had been useless since the first day out, and it remained useless, save for the compass. He had only a little power left on it, but enough to check the compass. He calculated the days and nights at sea and he calculated the wind and its strength and the number of days with and without wind and when he had finished his calculations he set his course with the aid of the compass. He bent to the engine and pumped the fuel bulb until he had resistance and the bulb was hard and the fuel bowl was full. He pulled out the choke. He paused, took the cord handle, and pulled. The engine started immediately. It screamed and shed blue smoke, and he pushed in the choke slightly and the engine settled and the smoke dissipated. He sat and listened to the engine putter. A beautiful sound. He shouted into the air. Stood and shook his fist at the sky. He sat and settled himself, pointed the boat south-southwest, and he set out.

THE MEN IN UNIFORMS who questioned him at the DNI in Tegucigalpa were called Chávez and Boquín and they were both in their thirties, and they both had straight white teeth and strong smiles. Chávez was the one who talked and he was talking now, leaning forward to speak, as if Quinn might be hard of hearing. He said that K., being a dead American, was of special interest and calls were being made and questions were being posed and the people at the American embassy had asked for a body, but it appeared that there was no body to deliver and how was this so? "Did you kill the American?" he asked.

"I did not," Quinn said. "He died of exposure."

"And you got rid of the body. Why do this? What were you hiding?"

"Nothing. I was hiding nothing. The body was decomposing and was stinking."

"But you threw the body overboard just before the *Carolina* arrived."

"I did not know the *Carolina* would be arriving. If I had known I would have not thrown the body into the ocean."

"How well did you know this American, K.?"

"A little. I took him out fishing three times in total."

"He was a rich man." This was a statement, not a question, but Quinn felt that it still required a response.

He said that yes, he believed K. was a rich man.

"How much did he pay you for the trip?"

"Two thousand."

"Dollars."

"Yes."

"Can anyone else verify this?"

"No. We were alone when he paid me."

"And so it might have been one thousand. Or five hundred. It is your word against the word of a dead man. Did you have any reason to kill him?"

"I didn't kill him."

"The question is only hypothetical. But necessary. Did the two of you have an argument?"

"No."

"Did this American, K., threaten you?"

"No, he didn't."

Chávez smiled. "He was a small man. We've seen your photographs. The ones you took. Why did you take them?"

Quinn did not speak for a time. Then he said that he had taken the photographs to prove that K. was dead. Because he feared that he would end up being interrogated. Which was now happening, and so his fears had proved to be quite real.

"But why be fearful if K. simply died of thirst and exposure? What was there to fear?"

"Not being believed," Quinn said. "I am a fisherman with a small boat. Mr. K. is an American businessman. So, you see?"

Chávez nodded in agreement. He understood, but this was not his job. He required the facts. He asked if Quinn's sister Clarita knew this man K.

"Briefly. A year ago."

"They were lovers?"

"I don't know."

Chávez shrugged. "Your sister said the same. She didn't know. How can she not know? Either they were, or they weren't."

"The man had many women. He talked constantly about them. About my sister, I do not know."

"But you do know about the ocean, yes? You know the boats, you know the winds, the tides, the dangers. You know the engines. How is it that, as you say in your testimony, the engine only started after the American died? How is it that you only built a sail from the tarpaulin after the American died? Why is this timeline so?"

Quinn knew there was no good answer but responded in a manner that might be credible. He said that there had been little wind, and therefore no reason to build a sail.

"And so, just after the American died, the wind picked up? Like a miracle?" Chávez asked.

"No. The motor finally started."

"Yes. It did. I see that." Chávez consulted the testimony. "But, for four days it will not start. And now, suddenly, it does."

"I found the problem," Quinn said, "Which was with the fuel jet."

"How much money did the American have in his wallet?"

"I didn't look."

"You didn't look."

Quinn waited.

"How much do you make a year?" Chávez asked. "Five thousand dollars?"

"If it is a good year. Yes. That is possible."

"The American's wallet was empty."

"I took nothing from his wallet."

"Who did then? The fish?"

"Perhaps it was empty when he came onto my boat. Perhaps the men who found me also found the wallet and took the money. I didn't."

"You see the problem presented here, no? We have a dead American and we have the man who saw him last and that man who saw him last is not dead, and so the question arises, how come you are not dead as well? How did this happen?"

"I was fortunate," Quinn said.

It was then that the other man, Boquín, spoke. His voice was rough, and it had a slight whine, as if he was impatient with the proceedings, or perhaps he was hungry and wanted to go out into the street to eat a hearty lunch. He said that the facts were such that there was not much of a leg for Quinn to stand on. "No legs, in fact, and there is no lawyer in this country who might argue for your innocence. There is no innocence here. Only guilt. I am sorry."

He was not sorry. It was only his manner of speaking. Quinn saw that there was nothing to be done. He asked for a drink of water. He thought of his two boys. Of Faustina. His head ached. His heart was heavy. When the water came, in a plastic cup, he took it. The water was warm and he drank it slowly, and when he was finished he set the cup on the table.

ON THAT SECOND to last day at sea, he had run the boat south-southwest, running out of fuel at noon, and so switched up the tank, and when the engine finally quit completely at dusk, he had covered a lot of ocean, but not enough to see land. He drifted in the darkness. The dead body had swelled in the sun and was certainly rotting from the inside. Quinn took down the remaining tarp and broke away the metal frame that had supported the tarp. He bent pieces of the framing and see-sawed them by hand until they broke and with the broken pieces he tied together a frame of sorts to which he attached the tarp with fishing line. And with this makeshift sail, he attempted to catch the winds blowing from the north. He found that he did not have enough hands and that the engine prop provided no purchase as a rudder and so he had to hold an oar within the crook of his arm, but in doing so he lost his grip on the sail. The boat went in circles.

At night the smell of the rotting body fell over him and he hung his head over the stern to catch the wind and to avoid the stink. By late afternoon the following day, with no prospect of salvation, it became necessary to throw the body overboard. With his phone he took a photograph of K. as proof of death. He took three photos in all—of the face, and the torso, and then of the body in its completeness. He found K.'s phone and wallet in his pockets. He took the sunglasses. He removed the wristwatch, a fat and expensive piece of equipment that could well survive beyond four generations of humans. He bound K.'s hands and feet. He wrapped the head in a tarp and fastened it at the neck with fishing line so that now the man resembled a prisoner going to the gallows. He drew the dead man's feet upwards over the gunnel and rested them there. He squatted and grasped K. beneath the armpits and heaved him upwards towards the gunnel and over. K. teetered for a moment and then slid into the water quietly, floated for a second, and then sank. Bubbles rose, and then more bubbles as the body receded and in the end there were no more bubbles. The body was gone.

At night he dreamed of a waterfall and in the waterfall there were children at play, swimming in the eddies of the pool beneath the falls, and the children were crying out, and they were speaking Spanish and the voices of the children grew deeper and the Spanish more singsong and louder and he woke to a bang against the fibreglass of his boat and so hearing he sat up, convinced that sharks were attacking. Before him a vision of a large fishing trawler whose name was painted in red, *Carolina*, and he saw a short man standing in the skiff, and the man spoke to him and asked him if he was alive, and when he said that yes, he was alive, the man spoke quickly, in the tones of a fisherman off the coast of Guatemala, for this is what he was, and Quinn recognized the language and the location of that particular accent and tongue and he said, "Soy Quinn."

"Venga," said the man, and he took Quinn by the elbows and pulled him up into his arms.

HIS BOYS WERE six and seven when he first told them the story of being stranded at sea. He had just been released from the federal prison north of Tegucigalpa. For five years he had waited for his case to go to trial, and then one day he had been informed that his case was finished. It was no more. And so he was set free. The scents of the island and the smell of his sons and the shape of his wife in his hands were marvellous and still new and hardly to be believed. He was diminished physically. But not mentally or spiritually. He had become stronger. He had learned to pray. Where it is darkest there is only hope, and that hope was achieved through talking to a god that he had needed during his time in prison. This was not sentimentalism or a deathbed conversion. He would not have called it a conversion. It was simply a manner of saving himself, just as fighting and cunning had been a path to survival.

When he told the story of the sea to the boys, he told it in a measured way, with little fanfare. He talked in great detail about the engine and its parts and he told them about the toothbrush and the copper wire and how the copper wire had been his salvation. He drew a picture of a fuel jet and within the centre of the jet he placed his sharp pencil and pressed down and then lifted the pencil and said that that little dot represented the tiny hole in the fuel jet and it was the hole itself that had been plugged, and so the fuel hadn't been able to flow, and not until he cleaned the hole with the copper wire that he so fortuitously had found, was he able to fire up the engine. The boys in their enthusiasm asked to have a drawing of the boat itself and so he accommodated them, and he drew a twenty-four-foot skiff with a tattered tarp and an engine at the stern. The boys asked for a drawing of their father inside the boat so as to locate their hero, and he drew himself hunkered over the engine. They asked if he had been alone on the boat, and he said that there had been another man, an American, but he had died. They were very curious about this man and asked why he had died and not Quinn. He said that he had been lucky. And he had been young. And again he said that luck had played a role. There were questions that they did not ask, and they could not know that these questions even existed. For these questions he had no good answers. Or he had many different answers. The boys asked if he had been frightened. He said that he had not been frightened. The ocean was there to feed them and to keep them and sometimes the ocean took back of its own accord. This they did not understand completely, but they listened and were silent and then, as if now tired of the story, they slid from their chairs and ran into the yard outside the house that they shared with their mother and father. Their voices at play were like the sounds birds make in the morning, when all is new and there is only time and more time for the day to unfold.

Here the Dark

A novella

As a child, Lily had a frequent dream in which she was getting into heaven via the front door. She knocked and God asked if she was skinny and she happily raised her dress to reveal that yes she was, and God looked her body up and down and said that she could enter, and so she dropped her dress and entered the place for which she had been destined. To show her bare body to God pleased her. One time, at Sunday lunch, she had heard that skinny people get into heaven quicker than plump people, and this being the truth, for it had come out of her uncle's mouth and he was a minister in the church, she studied herself in the mirror in the evening, before bed, making sure that she was still trim.

When she was thirteen, she gave her life to Jesus. On a Sunday afternoon, after she had announced her intentions, the deacons met with her and asked her three questions: had she made her confession, had she thrown away her school pictures, and was she willing to wear the head covering? She answered yes to all three questions, though in fact she had saved one of her school pictures. In the photo she was smiling happily. Her hair was in a single long braid. She was ten years old. She wore a blue printed dress with sleeves that came just below her elbows. Her mother had made the dress for her, after a trip to Ens Fabrics, where Lily had picked for herself the pattern of cloth that she most liked. Her father wore boughten clothes, purchased at Penner's at the strip mall, but the women of the family only wore handmade clothes, and for this they were grateful, for what is more sacred than that which is created by hand, the same hands created by the Maker. She kept the saved school picture in a blank envelope within a small box that was hidden beneath her white underwear in one of her dresser drawers in her bedroom. To tell a lie in such a manner filled her with some trepidation, but she was also aware, even at that age, that the lie excited her. She asked God for forgiveness for this trespass, and though God did not answer her, she felt that he understood. Or, she wished that he would understand, and in wishing this she convinced herself that he did.

Family, church, school, and work. This was the life of the Brethren. The life of a girl was to help the mother. With planting the garden, with cooking, with canning of fruits and vegetables, with caring for her baby sister, with plucking chickens, with pouring boiling water over the washed dishes, with setting the table, with polishing shoes. The polishing of the shoes was Lily's preferred job, for this was when she could be

alone, in the mud room, the shoes lined up on the wooden
worktable, the polishing cloth in her hand. She held one shoe
at a time in her left hand, and with her right she scraped up a
bit of polish and applied it and spread it about, covering the
scuffmarks, and a dull sheen appeared. And then, after the
shoes, four pairs in all, had been prepared, she set to buffing.
And in that buffing, elbows splayed, she saw each individual
shoe as a tiny soul, and she was like Jesus scrubbing the soul
clean. She never told anyone about this vision, for she was in
general a secret keeper. She did not divulge her fantasies, or her
doubts, or her imaginings, or her dreams. Her mother, who
always sang while she worked, worried constantly about her
little Lily, who might not be terribly bright because she didn't
answer when called to, and she always seemed to be staring off
into the sky, as if looking for the imminent second coming of
the Lord. But this was not Lily's reason for raising her eyes to
the heavens. She was, in fact, thinking of the world in its grand-
ness, and of the clouds that scuttled by, and one time she was
thinking of a question she had asked in school just the day
before, in which she had wondered about the parable of the
sower and the seeds that had been thrown onto the thorny
ground, and how it was that it might not be the fault of the seed
itself, which had no choice where it would land, and then she
had asked how it was that the farmer who had thrown the seeds
was not himself to blame? The teacher, Dorothy Plett, who was
not much older than eighteen, and was betrothed to be married
that June to Doug Bartlett, was befuddled by this odd and fearful question coming out of the mouth of a child, and so Dorothy
said that she would have to ask the deacons for the answer, for
she could not be certain. Dorothy said that it was dangerous to
question and it was dangerous to doubt, for questioning and

doubt were forms of sin and sin could only lead to hell. There was heaven above, and there was hell below, and it was certainly better to look up to heaven with your mouth zipped than it was to fall into hell with your mouth moving and calling out blasphemies. Well, this was not much of an answer for young Lily, who was far too intemperate for her own sake, as certain of the Brethren women who had witnessed her puffed-up pride liked to say about her. She was a wild horse and she would have to be broken. She would have to learn not to speak her thoughts. She would have to learn not to think. Lily frightened folks. She frightened her own parents. She frightened herself. Though, cleverly, and with a certain swelling in her chest, she liked the idea and feeling of being frightened by her own thoughts. Of course, being trained in the pitfalls of pride, she immediately prayed for forgiveness. But this didn't stop her, shortly after, from asking another impertinent question.

On the day of her baptism, her mother helped her into a newly made dress with a high collar, blue with white lilies, and hemmed just below the knee. In the bedroom, alone together, her mother whispered that she was happy for her. And then she recited a poem that was very familiar to Lily.

> Little drops of water,
> Little grains of sand,
> Make the mighty ocean,
> And the pleasant land.

And in that moment Lily felt her heart lift and she loved her mother and her father and she loved God and she loved the bride of Christ, which was the church. She was like a little drop of water that would be added to all the other little drops, and together they would make an ocean of love. She had to close her eyes so that she didn't faint from happiness. She breathed slowly. She opened her eyes. She saw her mother's face right next to hers, and she saw the shape of her eyebrows, and her ears, and she smelled her mother, always like cooking, and she saw the bits of grey in her hair, near her temples, and she said that she wanted to be just like her. This was true, in that moment, when her heart was full of love and generosity, but it wouldn't be how she would always feel, and as she grew older she would come to wish that she might be the opposite of her mother. For her mother was often tired, and though she didn't complain, she could have, given Lily's father's demands that supper be hot and on the table the moment he walked into the house, or that his clothes had to be laid out and washed and ironed each morning, or that the house be clean, and that the floors be polished, and the grass cut, and the walks shovelled in winter, and the laundry pressed and folded and put away, and the eggs gathered, and the canned pickle jars lined up neatly in the pantry, and, and, and. Or was this not her father at all, but her mother's need?

HER LIFE IN the Brethren Church was defined by the word *no*. No long hair on men. No voting. No education beyond Grade 8. No short hair on women. No military involvement. No political involvement. No divorce. No insurance. No parties. No dances. No trade unions. No hanging out at gas stations. No tobacco. No alcohol. No Santa Claus. No Easter bunnies. No snowmobiles. No birth control. No politics. No adult sports. No chrome on cars. No four-part singing. No bright colours. No cosmetics. No jewellry. No newspapers. No radios. No television. No novels.

This was Lily Isaac's world.

At the age of fourteen, she was deemed well enough educated and was therefore finished with school. One day, alone with her father and driving by the high school, Lily said, "I want to go there."

Her father said nothing.

This was a warm day in late fall, and classes were just letting out. The students fell through the school's doorways. Animals released. Girls standing in groups like tall birds, boys tumbling in the grass like dogs, a few slow and singular turtles, young couples kissing like doves. A conflagration of desire and violence. In her heart.

"I can be true," she said.

"It is impossible," her father said. "Ideas are strong and insidious."

"Ours or theirs?"

He looked at her then and his eyes were sad and she was sorry for her words. But only because he had heard them. She said that a tree, in order to thrive, needed a harsh wind.

"That," he said, pointing at the school, "Is a hurricane. We'll hear no more such talk, Lily. Your longings are of the devil. You must forsake them. Ask for guidance. For clarity."

She said that to pray was to ask for what was already evident. Prayer was the absence of knowledge.

"Where do you get these ideas?"

Because they had no books in the house, save for the Bible and Webster's Dictionary, it was to these two books that Lily went when she was famished for words. She would cast about for things to read, not truly understanding that she was looking, but looking nonetheless. One day at the doctor's office, when her mother went in for an examination, Lily had picked up a magazine. It was called *Reader's Digest*. She sped through it, and discovered Word Power, a quiz on vocabulary. She found that she knew all the words, and that her answers were always correct. She picked up another magazine called *Good Housekeeping*. And then another, with a young woman on the front in a bathing suit. She skimmed through the third one, alarmed at the photographs. But it wasn't the photos she was interested in. It was the words.

Over the next year, when she went into town and shopped at the fabric store with her mother while her father looked at augers and garden tractors at Loewen Farm Equipment, she sometimes snuck off to the doctor's office and spent fifteen minutes reading magazines. One time, because she was only half finished a story, she stole a *Reader's Digest* from the office. She went to the bathroom with the magazine and lifted her dress and stuck the magazine into her underwear, and she walked out of the bathroom and out of the doctor's office. All during the ride home she felt the sharp edges of the magazine against her stomach. She was horrified that she would be caught, and excited to get home to finish the article in the privacy of her room. She knew what she had done was sinful, but she rationalized that she would return the magazine when she next visited the office. And she did exactly this. And stole another magazine. And so it went, over that winter.

HER COUSIN MARCIE, who lived in town, and who was not a member of the church and was therefore free to participate in the world, she had books. These were often novels, and Lily, being curious, would pick up a novel when she visited Marcie and she would read quickly, sometimes thirty pages in one go, and when she went home she would leave the book at Marcie's house, and she would leave the strange comfort of Marcie's home. Marcie's mother, Aunt Dolores, barbecued hotdogs and she made noodles with a sharp cheese, and with the noodles she offered a Coke or 7 UP. These were all treats that Lily hadn't experienced at home. And there was the television, watched by Marcie's father, and sometimes Lily stood in the doorway, hiding, and watching. She liked best the advertisements, because they were so immediate and left her edged with longing for physical objects, and though this longing was urgent and full of ache, it also left her feeling slightly dirty.

When Lily turned seventeen, she began sewing herself dresses with darts that were a little too severe and so showed off the body underneath the dress, and she wore colourful underwear that Marcie had given her, and when she went to town she wore flip-flops instead of runners and so her feet were revealed to the outside world, and she was aware of Johan Gerbrandt in the Kleefeld church, whom she'd recently observed at the youth gathering, and she had been told by the other girls that Johan had noticed her as well. So it was. She didn't know what Johan Gerbrandt would make of her desires for reading. She knew that he drove a black Camaro. He had painted the chrome black as well, and he had removed the radio from the car. And she knew that he worked for his father on the farm, and that he was eager to marry. When she told her cousin Marcie about Johan, and about marriage, Marcie was horrified.

"You're too young, Lily," Marcie said. "You don't even know him."

"He's a good man," Lily said. "I've asked around. I'm of age."

"Have you talked to him?"

"Some."

"A tiny conversation isn't enough to know the man you'll spend the rest of your life with."

"My parents know his parents," Lily said.

"You're so naive. How do you even know if he's a good kisser?"

"Marcie. Shush."

Marcie, thinking that she had to inform Lily, convinced Lily to try on her jeans and blouses and bathing suit in the privacy of her bedroom. And after some arguing back and forth, Lily acquiesced, for the world was a large place, and Marcie's clothes were not her clothes. She was simply putting her toe into the water to test its temperature. Marcie had her try on her underwear as well, which was soft to the touch and revealing. In Marcie's mirror Lily studied herself and found that she might be attractive. She put on makeup and earrings. This was to die for. And then she removed everything and erased the outside world. But not quite. For Marcie had encouraged her to take home a book a week. With great trepidation, Lily agreed. She read at night, by flashlight. The stories were often ghastly, full of horrible people who slept with strangers who were not their spouses and deceived each other and lived in sin. Lily would read a chapter, throw it aside, pray for forgiveness, and the following night pick it up again. She had not read fiction before and so believed that everything in the story was true. Marcie laughed at her. What nonsense. "Of course it's not true. It's a story." Even so, Lily was not convinced, simply because the story had been so real. What followed were books that were no less ghastly, but invincibly compelling. Lily felt that she was making new friends, only these were friends who didn't know that she, Lily, existed. She read a novel about a young man who kills an old lady with an axe. She read the whole novel in one night, not sleeping, aware that the story was about the soul, and how the soul might be saved.

The deacons were most fearful of books, specifically fiction, and if they had asked Lily, she would have agreed, for novels set forth her imagination and took her to places she had never experienced, and they offered characters and descriptions of characters, but of course it was Lily who painted the final image of those characters. The possibilities were endless. Lily twisted the words and gave them new meaning and she twisted the descriptions of characters and she embellished their lives and the meaning that might be made of those lives. For example, she read that the young man who kills the old woman with the axe was "well-built with beautiful dark eyes and dark brown hair." But in her mind he was small and blond and dirty and not good-looking. He was Russian, and if he was Russian he must be blond, for her own descendants were Russian and blond, and her own descendants were stocky and they had rough faces and odd physical deformities. Like Frantz Gerbrandt, Johan's older brother, who was ugly, and who was, according to legend, wild and untamable. And so she created images that weren't at all faithful to the intent of the author. Did that matter? Not at all.

One day, in early fall, Marcie gave her a novel and told her that it was crazy and weird. She said there was a lot of sex in it, and she smiled.

Lily didn't mind sex, but she thought that too much was made of it, and she thought that the word itself was vulgar. She preferred 'having love,' or 'intercourse,' which was like a conversation. She had liked the Russian story best of all, and this was because there had been spiritual love rather than sex. She didn't say any of this to Marcie. She took the novel home and she read it through the night. She finished as the morning light was opening up the sky. She heard her father downstairs. She heard her mother's voice. She got up. She had in her mind now images of children drowning, and women sucking on penises, and men wearing dresses. The world of the book had been so foreign, so opposite, that she had been absolutely repelled by it and at the same time absolutely drawn to it. That morning, she left the book on the floor beside her bed.

ALL THAT DAY she made jam with her mother. They picked strawberries and they hulled and washed the berries and then Lily crushed the berries by hand and boiled them with sugar and pectin and poured them into sealer jars and poured hot wax over the jam in order to seal the jars, and then they screwed on the lids and wiped the sticky jars with a hot soapy cloth and dried them, and set the jars in rows on the kitchen counter. Late afternoon, she came in with fresh baskets of strawberries and on the dining-room table she saw the book. It was lying face down on the oilcloth. Her heart went wild and she paused and then, uncertain of what would happen next, she entered the kitchen. Her mother was skimming the foam from a fresh batch of jam. Spooning it into a white bowl. Lily carried on. Her mother said nothing. At supper, the book had disappeared. And still, nothing was said. She washed the dishes after supper, and then took her baby sister, Karen, out into the yard. Karen was three, a miracle baby she was called, and everything that could be done for her was done with awe and love. It was still hot and so Lily sat in the shade on an old wooden chair and she watched Karen toddle circles around her, her brown fat ankles sticking out from her dress. Lily had sewn the dress for Karen earlier that summer, from leftover cloth that Lily had used for one of her own dresses. The colours were a pale yellow and off-white and there were pastel bouquets of flowers in the pattern.

Lily's mind was scattered. She suspected that her father would open the book and study it. Her mother, she knew, would not touch it, and for this she was glad. Her mother was the harsher of the parents, more worried about the impressions of others, concerned about gossip and finger-pointing. Her father was more forgiving, in a rueful manner, but she also knew that her father couldn't overlook this trespass.

Dusk came. She gathered up Karen and carried her inside and boiled water for a bath. She poured hot water into the metal tub that sat on the kitchen floor. She added cold water and tested it with her wrist. Then she undressed Karen and sat her down in the tub. She scrubbed her back and soaped her little feet. Karen giggled and pulled away. She washed Karen's face and behind her ears. Karen fought. Lily persisted. Normally she would have made a game of this, the washing, the bath, the scrubbing, but on this evening she had no desire. When she had finished the bathing, she scooped Karen into a large blue towel and dried her. Carried her up to her bedroom and set her down and let her run naked around the room. It was too hot for pajamas. She considered the nakedness of childhood and she thought about the nakedness of adults, and she wished that she was once again a child. She tucked Karen into bed. They prayed together, Karen kneeling on the bed, Lily kneeling beside the bed. *In the evening, in the night, holy Jesus keep us light. If we pass before we wake, we pray thee please our souls to take.* When they were finished praying, she kissed Karen on the forehead and said goodnight.

Her parents were sitting at the dining-room table when she came down the stairs. Her Uncle Hans was there as well. The book was face up on the table. Lily paused in the doorway. Her father told her to sit with them. She did so. Her father pointed at the book and said, "What is this?"

"It is not mine," she said.

"Where did you get it?"

She did not answer.

Her mother sighed.

Her father picked up the book and opened it and read. The passage he had chosen was sexual and frank. Lily wondered how he had found that passage. Had it just opened to that page? When he finally halted, he placed the book on the table and he said, "How can this be edifying?"

Lily shrugged. She had no answer, or no answer that would have satisfied him.

"Have there been other books?" he asked.

She shook her head.

"Are you lying?" he asked.

She shook her head.

And then Uncle Hans spoke. His voice was softer than her father's and he said her name, "Lily," and then he said that ideas and images from the outside were forever dangerous, because those ideas worked from the outside to the inside and then back to the outside so that what were our thoughts now became our actions. "These are thoughts that seep into your soul," he said. "And it is impossible to remove them. They are like ink stains. They sit inside you and cannot be scrubbed away." He said that he would go outside and he would build a fire, and he wanted Lily to come out with the book, and together they would burn it.

"It's not mine to burn," she said.

"Whose then?"

She didn't answer.

Her father and her uncle rose and left the room and this left her with her mother, whose face was hard. "Filth," her mother said.

Was this true? Lily did not know. She wondered how it was possible to enjoy reading filth. For she had. And she hadn't. And then she realized that her mother was not referring to the book, but to her, Lily. She was filth.

In time, Lily stood and picked up the book and walked outside. The sun was setting. The light was soft and the sky was grey blue and the clouds were few.

The fire was burning in a half-barrel close to the barn. She approached her uncle, who stood alone and who gestured at the fire. Lily stepped forward and dropped the book into the flames. It did not burn immediately, for it was tightly bound, and even when it did begin to burn, the interior pages remained untouched, and so her uncle took up an iron rod and prodded at the book and he opened it so that the fire might attack all of it. During that time no words were spoken. There was just the action of her uncle spearing at the pages, and turning them, and offering them to the fire. Then it was finished, and only ashes remained. Her uncle turned and walked back to the house. Lily remained. She closed her eyes and when she opened them she looked for a sign that might perhaps arrive in the physical world around her.

And here the clouds like many dark sheep gone astray, and here the orange sun burning the world, and here the hare that hides from the circling hawk, and here the stretched singing of water-logged frogs, and here the light, and here the dark.

A T THE AGE of nineteen, she married Johan Gerbrandt after a short courtship that consisted of him visiting her at her family house where they sat in the living room and snuck looks at each other while the parents talked, and of her family going to the Gerbrandt home for Sunday lunch where roast beef, mashed potatoes, corn, and Jell-O was served. On those Sundays at his house, after lunch, she walked with Johan out to the yard. This was their time alone together. They sat in his car with the doors open and he told her his vision for his life. He would work the farm and eventually inherit the egg quota. He had an older brother, Frantz, who had the rights to the quota, but Johan said that Frantz was living a sinful life in the city and so he had lost his rights to the farm.

Johan walked her through the barn where the layers were kept. He walked her through the cooler where the eggs were stored. She liked the smell in the refrigerator room. She thought that she wouldn't mind working there. He showed her where he was building their house. The foundation had been poured. He said that they would marry when the house was finished. There would be three bedrooms for children, plus the master bedroom. He wanted four or five children, hopefully some sons to help him out on the farm. This was a confession that implied much of what he was dreaming of, in particular sex with Lily, and this being so, he turned red and looked away.

She said that she was looking forward to moving out of her parents' home.

"Is that all?" he asked. "You're using me to escape your family?"

"Oh, no." She laughed. "I am ready."

"I've watched you since you were fourteen," he said. "I told my friends that you were mine."

Okay. That was Johan, a very sure and certain man. He was big, and his hands were rough, and his beard, which was necessary for him to wear, was meagre and seemed to indicate a possible weakness. He wasn't weak though, this she knew. He was morally strong. He was soft with her. He paid attention. He was ready. More ready than she. The fact was, she didn't feel much about him physically, and when she did feel something it was often fear at what was to be. She couldn't imagine having relations with him. This absolutely frightened her. She thought that she was too skinny, and that he wouldn't like her body, and that she wouldn't know what to do with his big body. She spoke about all of this with Marcie, who advised her to take care of herself. "He'll be needy," Marcie said. "He'll have no idea what you want, and so you'll have to tell him."

"What do I tell him? I don't even know what I want."

"You want to feel safe, and you want pleasure," Marcie said. And she told Lily what an orgasm was, and how to achieve it.

"I don't know," Lily said. "It seems so selfish. If Johan's happy, I'll be happy."

"Don't worry, he'll be happy," Marcie said.

On that first Sunday, at the Gerbrandt's house, Lily had seen, as if in a singular vision, what her life would contain. And she was filled with happiness and immodesty. And she felt guilty for her happiness, and for feeling proud. On the eve of her wedding she slept in her single bed for the last time and as she dropped into her dream world she experienced the giddiness she had felt as a young girl when anticipating the slaughter of a hog.

THEY WERE MARRIED in the Grönland Church. Her Uncle Hans was the minister. There was no bridesmaid, and there was no best man, and so they stood alone, as a couple, in the front of the church. Johan couldn't stop himself from grinning throughout the service, and this comforted Lily. She paid attention to Johan's face and his smile and she tried not to lose sight of him throughout the afternoon. A meal was served in the church gymnasium: home-baked buns and bread, and butter with homemade strawberry jam, and farmer sausage, and coleslaw, and fruit punch that was served in plastic glasses, and there was a chiffon cake that she and Johan cut together, a cake that had been made by the women of the church. The children ran in circles while the men made speeches. There was no photographer, and so the only proof later of the wedding would be the witnesses, and the stories that might be told of the service, and the little bits of gossip, and the wedding dress that Lily had worn and which now hung in her closet in the master bedroom that she shared with Johan.

She discovered that she liked lying with Johan. She and Johan always had love in the evening right after supper, the dirty dishes abandoned on the dining-room table. They had love again, before bedtime, after the dishes were clean and the kitchen was put to rights. And they had love in the morning as well, after waking, and before Johan dressed for work and before Lily made his breakfast. Sometimes, during the day, he would appear in the dining room where she might be sitting at her sewing machine, and when she heard his heavy step, her body would rise up, for she knew what was to come. She followed him upstairs to the bedroom where he undressed and then lay on the bed and waited for her to undress and lie down beside him. He never attempted to unbutton her dress and remove it, or to kiss her before suggesting that they lie together, for this is what he called it, and though she was perhaps happy that he did not interfere in this way, she imagined that a prelude to lying together, touching and kissing, might make it all even more enjoyable. When they had love during the day, when the sun was high in the sky and the light in the bedroom flattened the walls and the bed and the objects in the room, she undressed in the bathroom and removed her kerchief and let out her hair and came to him wrapped in a towel, and she climbed under the covers, and only then did she remove the towel. Sometimes, he took the time to pull back the covers and admire her body and to touch her, and to stroke her hair that fell below her waist. When he was done, he went to the washroom and returned to put on his clothes, and as he dressed he spoke to her of the farm and the chickens and he spoke of manure and the blend of the feed and sometimes he told her what he would like for supper, though this was rare, for he was usually happy with what she prepared for him.

She thought that she might want more from him. He was not rough with her, but neither was he tender, and she felt at times that he lay with her in the same way he ate. To fill a space inside of himself. In fact, there were times when she sat across from him and watched his face and she imagined his mouth between her legs, and thinking that thought she laughed inside. How strange. She thought of the books that she had read, and she thought of the passions that the female characters had experienced, and she realized that Marcie had been correct when she had said that novels were not true, that they were simply made-up stories about people who did not exist and who had never existed.

One evening, determined to try something new, she lit candles in the bedroom and she wore a chemise that Marcie had given her as a wedding present, and she put herself on the bed and waited for Johan to appear. The chemise was black with lacy edges and it was short and when she lay on top of the quilt her thighs were visible and her arms were bare and her hair, combed out, lay beneath her. When Johan appeared and saw the flickering candles and saw his wife in the new chemise and saw her bare legs, he paused.

"Are you okay, Lily?" he asked.

He sat on the bed. She took his hand and put it up under her chemise, between her legs. She held his hand there. He turned his head away.

"It's okay," she said. "I won't hurt you."

She began to unbutton his shirt. And then loosened his buckle. She told him to undress. He did so.

When he lay down beside her she touched his penis. She had never done this before but he did not object. She kissed him with an open mouth. This too he allowed. She whispered in his ear, "Put your mouth on me. Down there."

"Where?"

"Here," she said, and pushed his hand between her legs. She moved his head down towards her stomach and she shifted upwards. She expected him to revolt, but he didn't. He went down, and when she shifted his head with her two hands he allowed this, and when she gave him further instructions, he obeyed. She did not know for sure what to expect, but she felt wild and when she pulled him upwards and he was inside her she clawed at his back, and later, when he was finished and he was walking to the bathroom, she saw the red marks on his shoulder blades.

He wanted to pray. He said that he felt a need for forgiveness.

"For what?" she asked.

"It was abnormal," he said.

"You didn't like it?" she asked.

"I did. But still."

And so he prayed, and he asked her to pray as well, but she said that she didn't want to pray. She had nothing to say. She got up and blew out the candles. She went to the bathroom and removed the chemise. She brushed her hair, facing the mirror. She wondered if Johan wished for bigger breasts. Or if he wanted a rounder body. She was not yet pregnant, and it had been six months since the marriage. He was waiting, this she knew. As was her mother, and Johan's mother. The whole world was waiting.

She left the bathroom, turned out the light, and crept in darkness towards the bed.

She climbed in, and lay on her back.

Johan was sleeping.

SHE WANTED TO help out on the farm and so insisted that she would gather the eggs in the morning and the late afternoon. Her job required that she walk the cement walkways between the cages of chickens and gather the eggs that had rolled down into the metal troughs beneath the cages. She gathered the eggs three at time in each hand, and placed them in the flats that lay on her cart. Sometimes the eggs were still warm, and sometimes they were streaked with blood and shit. At the end of the row, she turned her cart and proceeded down the cement walkway in the opposite direction. When her cart was full, she went to the refrigerator room and stacked the flats, which were full of eggs, and then returned to the barn to gather more eggs.

One afternoon, she said that she wanted to visit her friend Marcie in town, and would she be able to use the Camaro. Just for an hour.

He did not say anything and she wasn't sure if she'd been heard. Then she said that if he preferred she could use the pickup instead, she didn't mind. He said that the pickup was fine, but not to wander, for gas was expensive.

It was August, and Lily knew that Marcie was moving to the city to attend university, and she wanted to see her before she left. She rode the number 52 from Kleefeld and she drove fast with her windows down so that the summer air came in and so she could see more clearly the last combines in the field gathering up the harvest. There was dust in the air, and there were dark clouds to the south, and some of the clouds looked like funnels, and Lily imagined a tornado sweeping down and carrying away the chicken barn and the layers and all the eggs and Johan and his family.

They sat in Marcie's bedroom, as in the old days, and they talked of Marcie's new apartment, and of Marcie's breakup with her boyfriend, who hadn't understood why there was a need to break up, and how Marcie had told him that she was leaving him because she wanted to. "He was very sad," Marcie said, "but he wouldn't have understood me otherwise. I had to be mean about it." Lily saw that Marcie felt for him, but not enough, obviously, for Marcie was mostly happy for herself. Marcie asked how married life was, and Lily knew what she was referring to, but she just said that it was good, it was normal, and they moved back to Marcie and her excitement and her desires. "I won't come back," Marcie said, and Lily believed her, and she wondered what that would be like, to not come back.

Marcie offered her books, insisted that Lily take them. One in particular was vital because it was about a woman who realizes that men just want her eggs and she herself stops eating eggs. "It's an important book," Marcie said.

"I'd just read it and then burn it," Lily said.

"What are you talking about?"

And so, as if she might be relating the plot of one of the stories she'd read, Lily told Marcie how her uncle had burned a book with her. And then she described how she had continued to borrow Marcie's books, and some of these she had burned as well, on her own. She said that with each book she read, she was sometimes elevated and she was often disgusted and if she was disgusted she burned the book. Read a book, burn a book. "I'm sorry, Marcie," she said.

"That's crazy," Marcie said.

"Yes. And that's why you shouldn't give me any more books. Anyways, I've decided that reading is a waste of time. What good is it? Does it make jam? Does it hoe the beets? Does it wash the clothes? Does it make babies? Does it get you to heaven? It just makes you unhappy."

Marcie laughed. "Oh, Lily. What will I do with you?"

ONE SUNDAY AFTERNOON, she and Johan drove up to Sandilands for a wiener roast with Eleanor and Jimmy Krahn, another newlywed couple from the church. Jimmy was a good friend of Johan's. Lily was acquainted with Eleanor, and they might have gotten along, except right off Eleanor announced that she was pregnant, and so this fact clouded Lily's day. While the men wandered off into the bush to gather firewood, Lily and Eleanor sat on stumps and slapped mosquitoes and Eleanor talked about the baby. She asked if Lily was pregnant yet, and Lily said that she wasn't. It would come of course. In good time.

Around the fire later, Eleanor talked of her cousin Irmie, in Kansas, who at twenty-two had left her husband and two young children and moved to California and was living with a movie director and might even be acting. Eleanor said the word acting with much disdain and great force. Lily was curious about Irmie. She was amazed at the audacity and bravery and foolhardiness and insanity of a mother who would leave an infant and a two-year-old and run off to shack up with a movie director and to bare herself before him and to forsake everything to which she had committed. What slippery thinking did that take? She asked Johan later what he thought of Irmie running off like that.

"It's not something I want to talk about, Lily," he said. "And not something you should talk about either. There is nothing edifying in it."

And so she let it go.

But still, when in the barn gathering eggs, or when preparing herself for church, or even sitting in church as the preacher spoke, she found her mind floating sideways to the lives of others, and in particular to the life of Irmie, who certainly couldn't be happier now with her new existence.

And so Lily began to wonder if she, Lily, had chosen her life, or if that life had simply fallen into her lap, as it had fallen into her mother's lap, and her father's lap, and Johan's lap. She looked at the women in the church, and she studied the men across the aisle, and she watched the children, and she observed the young mothers with their infants, and in all of them she saw peace and happiness and love and joy and she wondered if she had peace and joy. She thought yes. She loved Johan. She liked being with him when he was around, even when she was sewing and he was in the next room sleeping in his chair like an old man. What wasn't there to love? Still, when she had heard the little bit of gossip about cousin Irmie, she had jumped sideways. A light had peeked through the heavy foliage of the trees that was Lily's existence, and the light had landed on her face and on her chest, and it had warmed her.

ON A MONDAY MORNING, she took the pickup into town and went to the doctor's office and she sat in the stillness of the small waiting room, and when her name was called, she entered the doctor's office. There were posters on the wall, images of skeletons and organs, and there was a pamphlet that spoke of the beauty of birth and the life of a child from conception. She was reading this pamphlet when the doctor came in and closed the door. She knew Doctor Giesbrecht. Her mother had taken Lily to see him when Lily had contracted measles. He was a pleasant man, in the manner that an uncle at a family gathering might be pleasant—full of jokes and a wet mouth and perhaps a little too much attention paid. Lily spoke immediately of her concern, that she wasn't yet pregnant and she wanted to be pregnant.

Doctor Giesbrecht asked if Lily's husband knew of this visit.

"No, he's not aware," Lily said.

The doctor nodded. He took her blood pressure. He asked her to lie on the bed and to remove her underwear. She did so, and closed her eyes. She heard the snap of a glove going on. He said that she might feel a touch of coolness. He told her to raise her knees. She obeyed. When he put his fingers inside her she imagined that this was Johan standing above her, and this helped. The doctor stepped back and told her that she should stand and remove her dress. He was now leaning against the far wall and he was waiting. She stood and removed her dress. He said that she should also take off her bra. She did so. She did not look at him. She was staring at the poster that named the organs of the body. He asked her to raise her arms above her head. She did so. He asked her to turn around and face the opposite wall. She did so. It was quiet and she didn't know what to do and she was aware that he was three steps away from her and that only Johan and Marcie had ever seen her naked, but she reasoned that he was a doctor and that this was necessary. Finally, he told her to get dressed. He left the room and was gone for a long time, and when he finally returned, Lily was sitting on the chair, dressed and waiting. He stood before her and consulted a chart and he did not look her in the eye. He said that everything seemed normal. She was young, and she was healthy. He asked her how often she had relations. She lied and said twice a week. He asked if any protection was used. She didn't understand. Birth control, he said. "Does your husband use a condom? Are you on the pill?"

She laughed and said, "Oh no, oh no."

He said that time would tell. She was young and beautiful and her body was ripe.

She didn't understand why he used the word ripe. It brought to mind a banana aging on the kitchen counter. She asked that he not tell anyone about this visit. She didn't want Johan or her mother-in-law to know.

He said that everything about the visit was private. There was no one to tell. It was her body. He said again that she was very beautiful, and to this she had no answer.

That evening, while lying with Johan, she saw herself in the doctor's office, facing the opposite wall, her back and buttocks bare, and she was horrified that Johan would find out what she had done. She prayed that no one would discover her trespass.

A YEAR PASSED. The seasons spun around like the Lazy Susan on Johan's mother's dining-room table. Fall, winter, spring, and then the heat of summer. She was still barren, and because of this a great disappointment settled over the house and space she shared with Johan. They had love less often. Johan was not interested, or if he was interested he did not show it. She sometimes forced herself on him, as if this might assuage the guilt she felt, but the act was dutiful and desultory. She took to feeding him large and special meals, and it was as if these meals had now replaced the lack of a child. He ate mightily and then lay down on the couch and slept while she did the dishes, and then he woke and climbed the stairs to the bedroom, and later in the evening, when she joined him, he was again fast asleep. She thought that they had, already at such a young age, become old and tired.

Marcie invited Lily for a visit and so on a Friday afternoon, Lily took the pickup and went to visit her cousin in the city. She had always loved the movement towards the city by vehicle, the strip of highway, the initial sighting of the tall buildings of Winnipeg, the confluence of ever more traffic so that she nearly panicked, the shopping malls, the people on the streets, the smell of exhaust from the buses, the sense that she was insignificant. Marcie lived on Kennedy, in a one-bedroom apartment, and immediately, upon entering the apartment,

Lily felt herself relax. Marcie played music and she burned incense and she smoked Du Maurier cigarettes and she wore clothes that were modern and of the fashion. Marcie drank red wine and Lily drank tea. Marcie talked about her life, and she talked about the courses she was taking. She told Lily that she was a feminist and she said that women had to take back the space that men had stolen from them. She talked about her body. She talked about ownership. She said that she was proud of her period, and Lily thought that this was the oddest thing to be proud of. She herself wasn't ashamed of it, but she hadn't ever thought it worth discussing. Lily realized that Marcie was like an alien who now came from a completely different world. It was very late when Lily said that she had to drive home, and Marcie said that she should stay the night.

"Oh but Johan," Lily said. "I have to make him breakfast."

"He won't die if you stay," Marcie said.

And so she phoned Johan and told him that she would drive home early in the morning. He sounded sleepy, and he didn't argue with her. He asked if she was behaving herself.

"Of course," Lily said. "I'm with Marcie."

"She's of the world," he said.

Lily ignored this, said that she loved him, and she said goodbye.

She and Marcie shared a bed and during the night Lily woke and felt the beating of her own heart and she heard, through the open window of the apartment, people passing by and talking late at night, and the voices were male and female, out at night, and no one seemed shrill or anxious, and there was laughter and then loud discussion, and the voices passed on and Lily wondered how it was that one person was this way, and another person was that. It was not her first moment of doubt. She had suffered misgivings before, but she had always pushed those doubts aside. They were of the devil. They were sinful. They were thorns. But now, in the darkness of the room, lying beside Marcie, she felt the thorns quite deeply and she sensed that these thorns might be speaking to her. She wiped her eyes and cheeks. Her heart ached, but she did not know why.

In the morning she arrived home to find Johan in the barn. She found him and kissed him on the cheek and then she put on coveralls and she gathered eggs. She made him a lunch of egg salad and she thawed a loaf of whole wheat bread that she had made the week previous. She put out butter and fresh jam and pickles. They ate silently. She tried to tell him of Marcie's life, but he was not interested. She tried to use the word feminism, but he would not hear of it.

At one point he asked, "Do you want her life?"

She turned red and shook her head, but even the question itself, coming from his mouth, indicated a betrayal on her part.

TO CHANGE, TO DECIDE to shift away from the beliefs of one's upbringing, is never a sudden decision. Most change is gradual, and so it was with Lily. She felt hollow, and the hollowness was like when one has fasted and gone without food for a long time, and the hunger one feels becomes deep and acute, and then, after a time, the pangs disappear and they remain as a dull memory and the body gets used to it. But also, as with someone who starves, the skin becomes thinner and the bones are visible, and if the light falls on the hand at a certain angle, the translucence of the body is shocking, and the flesh becomes nothing, and it is as if you are invisible. Sometimes, on a winter morning, after Johan had left the house, she stood by her bedroom window and looked out onto the snow that covered the yard and that had swept up against the windbreak of trees beyond the chicken barn. The land was flat and she could see forever, and the light was blue and sharp and it reflected off the miles of snow that covered the fields, which resembled a desert, though she didn't truly know what a desert looked like. She had only seen pictures. Within six months, she was no longer going to church. She spent Sunday mornings reading novels that she had picked up at the town public library. She had gone there one day and asked how to borrow books and she had been given a library card and the first time she had only taken one book, a novel chosen at random, and when she learned that she could check out as many books as she liked, she signed out ten and took them home and stacked them by her bed. She was more brazen now with her books. She left them on the night table, or in the living room, and when Johan picked one up and turned it around in his hands, he did so as if it was an offending and mysterious object. He did not understand the allure. Or he understood it very well.

Every weekday morning at ten, always at ten, Johan's mother Elmira entered the house without knocking or calling out. She looked like a root vegetable, a parsnip that had been uprooted during an early harvest and left abandoned to the heat of the day and the cold of the night, and had shrivelled. She suffered back problems, and this being so she shuffled around Lily's kitchen and the dining room with her head curled towards the ground, as if looking for some object that might have dropped, a pickle perhaps, or a fork that might have slid off the table. The effect was such that Lily inevitably also bent her head towards the ground to seek out that pickle or that fork. Finding nothing,

Elmira moved through the rooms, now seeking dust, or a chair out of place, or a plant that might be dry, or a dirty tablecloth. When she found fault, she corrected it. She did not speak, she would just look sour and tssk, and then she would water the dry plant, or she would get out the dusting supplies and spray Lemon Pledge and scrub at the coffee table, or she would remove the offending tablecloth and replace it with a clean one, taking home the dirty laundry to wash it herself. Rumour was that Lily was not a good housekeeper. She was sloppy. She did not have a passion for spotlessness. The fault of this might have fallen onto Lily's mother, who had not trained Lily well, but in this case the fault for all the disorder was blamed on books. One day, Mrs. Gerbrandt said, just before stepping out of the door to return to her own gleaming house, "All these books are making your home dirty." Mrs. Gerbrandt was breathless, and her hands were shaking, and her mouth moved but no more words came out. For a brief moment Lily felt for her. The word that came to mind was apoplexy, which could mean stroke or extreme anger. It wasn't clear which one Mrs. Gerbrandt might be suffering. In order to help, or perhaps to be free of her, Lily walked her across the yard to her own house and by the time they had reached the door, Mrs. Gerbrandt had recovered and she was saying to Lily, "Come back. Come back. I see all sorts of tribulation."

Lily held Mrs. Gerbrandt's elbows and looked her directly in the eyes and said, "I am no different than before. There is no tribulation."

THE ELDERS PAID Lily a visit on a Sunday afternoon. They spoke to her of her duties as a wife and as a member of the church, which was the bride of Christ. They read Bible verses to her and they prayed with her. They did not ask for permission, they just said that they would now pray, and they did. She kept her eyes open as they prayed and she looked at their hands and their bearded faces and she looked at their black shoes, which needed polishing, and she studied their slacks and their pressed shirts with no ties, and she found that she was cold and indifferent.

Rumours arrived that Lily Gerbrandt, née Isaac, would be excommunicated from the Brethren Church. And then one day the rumours came true, and the elders again arrived and told her that because she was no longer attending church, and because she was reading secular novels, and because she was acting out of rebellious pride, she would be dismissed from the church. She would no longer be allowed to eat with her husband, and she would no longer be allowed intimacies with her husband. If she should repent of her sins she would be allowed back into the church. Until that time, all rules of excommunication would apply.

When the men were done talking she asked them if Johan was in agreement. They said that they had spoken with Johan and he was aware. She was ashamed, for she had thought that Johan would be against this type of meeting, and these kinds of words. She lifted her head and said that she had done nothing wrong. There was nothing to repent.

The last word was left to one of the men, a younger fellow called Raymond, with a sparse beard and very red lips who when he spoke spit out his words as if those same words had left a bad taste in his mouth. He said that pride was the ultimate sin, and that she, Lily, suffered from a vast and unholy pride that would be her downfall. And then the men left.

That night she made homemade noodles and farmer sausage and she made Johan's favourite gravy, drippings of the sausage mixed with heavy cream, and she boiled carrots and added butter and brown sugar. When Johan came in, he looked at the table and the two settings, and he went into the mud room and came back with a smaller table and he set that table next to the kitchen table, making sure that the tables were not touching. One for him, the other for her. He ate in silence. She did not. She talked about her shame, not for herself, but for the two of them, and she said that nothing should come between them, not even the church. He did not respond. He finished eating and he rose and went upstairs. She cleaned up and did the dishes and when she climbed the stairs to go to bed, she saw that Johan had made for her a bed in one of the empty bedrooms. He had put on clean sheets, and there was a clean down comforter, and two pillows, and there were towels laid out at the foot of the bed, and she was aware that he had never before made a bed or put on sheets or smoothed a comforter. He did not do domestic things. And yet, here he was, tenderly preparing a bed for her, and it was as if she were a guest in her own house.

SHE WAS LONELY. Her mother and father were required to stop talking to her, and the only way they communicated was through Marcie's mother, Aunt Dolores, who, because she was not a member of the church, was allowed full access to the shunned Lily. Aunt Dolores arrived one day with a bag of Liquorice All Sorts, and they sat in the kitchen that no longer felt like Lily's kitchen and they drank tea and ate the sweets and Aunt Dolores said that Lily's mother still loved her, and even though they could not speak, she spoke to her in her head all the time. "Your mother said that you should straighten your ways, Lily. She said that you have a stubborn heart. That your head is wobbly."

"Ha," Lily said. "That is the thistle calling the dandelion a weed."

Aunt Dolores smiled.

"What do you think, Aunt Dolores?" Lily asked.

Her aunt sighed. She said that it was all very sad, and that there were too many rules, and the rules had replaced any semblance of love.

Lily heard the word semblance, and this revived her for some reason, as if a single word could lift her up.

Aunt Dolores said, "Marcie, by the way, thinks that you should leave. I told her that it was impossible. What would you do? Where would you go? She said that you could live with her, in the city. I said that you wouldn't. I said that you were married."

Lily said that she wasn't allowed to eat with Johan. Or to speak to him. Nor were they allowed to sleep together.

"He's a man. I can't imagine him lasting very long," Aunt Dolores said, and laughed, as if the ways of men and boys were simple and straightforward.

Lily said that Johan was incredibly stubborn. And that he could be mean in his withholding. And that his mother and sisters were equally stingy and mean, and wouldn't even look at her, let alone talk. To all of this Aunt Dolores said little. She simply sighed and said that it was all too mad.

AND THEN ONE evening at supper Johan spoke to her. It was the first time in weeks, and when she heard his voice she trembled and tears came to her eyes and she thought that it was over. But it wasn't. He simply announced that she wasn't to use the pickup or the Camaro. They were no longer hers to drive. She asked how she would get milk and groceries from town. He said that his mother would buy the groceries. He said that if she needed something, anything, she should write a list and leave it on the kitchen counter and he would pass it on to his mother.

She was mute.

And then she asked if he missed her. "I miss you," she said.

He shook his head and said that the talking was done.

She said that he might be done talking, but she wasn't. And she said that she had married him because she loved him. She still loved him. She missed him. She said that she missed having sex with him. She used the word sex and she saw that he lifted his head to look at her and then he turned away. She said that the church was wrong to come between them. "That is not the way of love," she said. "That is not the way of kindness. This is the way of darkness."

He said that it was she who had chosen the darkness. It was she who had sinned. He had simply wanted to be with her in a normal way, as his mother and father had lived, as her mother and father had lived. He had no longings. No wishes. No desires but the simple and plain ones he had been raised with. "It is you who wants more. Not me."

She did not answer for a long time. And then she said, "But what if there is more? What if this life here, our life, is only half a life?"

"It isn't. It is a full and correct life. And this is your sin, not mine."

She said his name then, and reached for his hand, and he let her hold it.

That night, she moved from her own bed in the guest room and crawled into Johan's bed, the bed that used to be both of theirs. He woke. He asked what she was doing. She was naked and she let him know this. He did not speak, and when she touched him he turned towards her and pushed his hands up along her ears so that his fingers were tangled in her hair. He moaned and said that this was wrong. And then they had love. She slept with him that night, throwing her leg over his hot body and clamping him to the bed. They had love again in the morning. She talked to him at breakfast. And he talked back. They laughed together. They were laughing and talking when his mother walked into the kitchen. When he saw her he went silent. His mother turned and left the house.

FOR SUPPER SHE made beef borscht and angel biscuits and a gingerbread cake for dessert that she would serve with whipping cream. When he came in from the barn he washed his hands at the kitchen sink and dried them with a tea towel and he sat down. When she sat down across from him he got up and moved to the second table. She asked him how his day was but he did not answer. She knew that his fierce and formidable mother had spoken to him. Lily, in order to match that fierceness, ignored Johan's silence and she talked about her day, of which there was little to say, but regardless, she still talked. She said that she had used the last of the ground beef from the freezer, and they would have to buy more. She said that the potatoes in the cellar were growing eyes and those at the bottom of the barrel were beginning to rot. She said that she would clean the barrel tomorrow and assess their stores. She said that it was fortunate that she had frozen the fresh dill in fall, so that now she could just dip into the freezer for what was the closest thing to fresh dill. The parsley she'd used was dried, however, as all the fresh frozen parsley had been used up. She said that she needed new underwear, and she didn't think that his mother would want to buy her dainty things. She said that she had enjoyed being with him the night before. "I was so happy," she said. "And you were too. I could tell." To all of this, he did not respond. He ate his soup, and he squeezed Roger's Golden Syrup over his steaming biscuits, and he drank a tall glass of milk in one go and poured another. She did not touch her own food. She simply talked and watched him, and she knew that he was listening.

It became a habit of theirs that at meals he would eat and she would talk. He never told her to stop talking, but neither did he respond or open his mouth to speak. She had moved beyond talking about the practicalities of the house, the objects in the fridge, her daily life, to talking about emotions. She said that she felt invisible. "I know that I'm not supposed to feel anything, but I am very lonely. At least I think I am lonely. It is in my chest." And she moved her hand towards her chest and then away again. She said that even now she was lonely, even though she was talking. She was young. Too young to be so sad and alone. And it was on that day, in the late afternoon when he had come in for his nap on the couch, that she introduced death. She told him about an eight-month-old child who had crawled out the door one summer evening and made his way out to the pasture and was lost to the family. Presumed dead. She said that the family hunted high and low. The mother spent her nights weeping. The father was heartbroken and avoided the mother of the child, whom he blamed for leaving the door open. But, in fact, it had been the father who had left the door ajar. This the mother knew, but she said nothing to contradict the father. The loss of the child moved through their lives. The father, whose name was Frank, in his grief suggested another child. The mother was horrified. So soon. So soon. But Frank insisted, and so they set about to create another child. The mother's heart was abject and because her heart was abject her body rebelled. It spurned pregnancy.

But the child was not dead. It had been lucky enough to be picked up by a passing wolf and was carried back to the lair and raised by the wolf, a female, and her male partner. Five years passed. Litters came and went. The child walked about on all fours. It loped like a wolf. It spoke wolf language. It ate raw meat. The child, of school age now, was discovered by a farmer out hunting, who killed the mother wolf and scooped up the child. The child, who spoke only wolf language, and knew only the ways of a wolf, and was a meat eater through and through, was returned to the family, who had to lock the boy up at night because he was feral and dangerous. The boy couldn't speak, he had no words, he just grunted. Even so, she said, the family was happy to have him back.

She stopped talking. Then she said that Johan must be tired. She said she was planning on making noodle casserole and corn on the cob and boiled beets for supper.

That night she heard him moving about in his room, and then to the bathroom, where he ran water for the longest time, and then back to his room. She heard him climb into bed. He sighed. He was already old, or acted old, and therefore seemed older than he was. She missed him. She picked up a book and she opened it. The lamplight was yellow and the words wavered and bent. The story was an old one, given to her by Aunt Dolores, who had little sense of taste, but threw novels at Lily like a lifeline. Here, and here, and here. And she snatched at them, and clung to them, and if the lives of the people she read about were harder and more dire and more desperate and sadder than her own, this did not make her happier, and it did not bring about any release, for she was buried deep beneath the soil of her upbringing, and it would take more than words to extract her.

SHE DID NOT know that she was pregnant until she lost the baby. Six months earlier, when she and Johan had still been sharing a bed, she had missed a period and she had been sure that she was pregnant, and then her period resumed and she was relieved that she hadn't said anything to Johan. This time she had gone two months without a period, but she hadn't been with Johan, except for that one time, and so she assumed that pregnancy was impossible. Only in hindsight did she recall her mood swings—extreme happiness, and then extreme sadness. Or the thickness in her body—thinking she was losing her shape, she had tried to eat less, but often woke at night ravenous and climbed downstairs to pour milk over a large bowl of cereal and when she had finished, eat toast.

One evening, as she was peeling potatoes and dropping them whole into the pot of cold water on the counter, she felt a pain in her lower back and then it went away and came again, except this time it was very sharp and lasted a long time, and so she bent over, holding the paring knife in her hand. When the pain was gone she saw blood on the floor between her feet, and she lifted her dress right there in the kitchen and pulled down her underwear and she saw that she was a mess. She went to the bathroom and she locked the door and removed her dress and underwear and she sat on the toilet and she hemorrhaged. She was weak from loss of blood, and she had difficulty standing. She knew by now that she had probably been pregnant, and when she stood she looked down into the toilet bowl, fearful of what she would see, but all she saw was blood and clots of other matter. She managed to wrap a towel between her legs, and she washed herself, and then took the blood-soaked towel and placed it in a garbage bag, and she stuck a clean smaller towel between her legs and fetched some large underwear that would keep the towel in place, and she put on a larger dress, clean as well, and she stuffed the soiled dress and underwear into the garbage bag that held the bloody towel and she tucked the garbage bag under a shelf to be dealt with later. She sat in the kitchen for a long time, at the table, her head in her hands. She could still smell the blood and she wondered if Johan might smell it as well when he came in for supper. She rose and cut the potatoes and put them on to boil, and she checked the chicken roasting in the oven, and she opened a tin of corn, and cut some tomatoes and laid them on a plate. Throughout all of this she felt faint and had to sit down several times.

At supper, it was quiet as usual. She would normally have talked, have described her day for Johan, and talked about her thoughts and musings, but tonight she had nothing to say, for she didn't have any words to say about what had happened to her, and any other topic would have been an abhorrence. She was afraid. Johan ate stoically and glanced up at her now and then, as if surprised by her silence, as if he indeed missed her voice, but he said nothing, for that was his duty, and when he was done, he pushed back from the table and went into the living room and lay down on the couch.

She cleaned up, shuffling from the table to the sink with the dirty dishes, the towel rubbing between her legs. She deboned the chicken and threw the carcass into a Dutch oven and added celery and onions and a bay leaf and salt and pepper, and then she filled the pot with water and set it to boil. This would be soup stock. She felt weak and had to sit briefly. When she rose again, she went to the bathroom and locked the door and lifted her dress and checked the towel between her legs. The blood had eased, but this towel was ruined as well, and she stuffed it into the garbage bag and found a newer and smaller and less cumbersome towel and she placed it between her legs and pulled up her underwear and dropped her dress and went out into the kitchen to finish the dishes.

Later that evening she built a bonfire in the drum in the yard out back and when it was burning hotly she fetched the garbage bag from the bathroom and she dragged it out to the fire and she threw the towels one by one onto the fire where they were slowly consumed. Her underwear and dress went last, and these caught quickly and flared and then disappeared. When she turned from the fire she looked back at the house and saw that Johan had been watching her from the kitchen window. When she came into the house, she heard him upstairs, and she did not see him again until the morning, when he came down for breakfast.

She waited for him to speak, to ask her why she had burned towels and dresses, but he said nothing and she thought then that he was completely lacking in curiosity or that he was guided by rules that were so misshapen that he no longer understood who he was, or who she was, and she felt great pity for him.

That afternoon she was weak and she was still cramping and so she climbed the stairs to her bed to nap. She fell asleep with the autumn sun warming her feet. And she woke with the horrific thought that she had introduced death into the house through her own words. She realized that she could not tell Johan or anyone else about the miscarriage. If he asked, she would deny it. And so she was alone with this, as she was alone with her other thoughts and her questions. She had no sense of what had happened to her physically, except to understand that she had bled out a baby. She didn't know why her body had acted in this way. She thought that it might be God punishing her for her stubbornness, and for her love of fiction, and for having pushed Johan's head down between her legs that one time, and for having seduced him when he was not to touch her, and so she imagined that she was to blame. She prayed for forgiveness, but she felt no sense of release. She no longer had access to the Camaro or the pickup, and so she no longer had access to the library, where she might go to look up books on pregnancy. She had no wish to go to see Dr. Giesbrecht, who would have her stand naked with her face to the wall while he studied her from behind. To what end?

Two days later, still spotting and weak, she called Aunt Dolores and told her what had happened. Aunt Dolores drove out immediately. She entered Lily's home and came straight up to the bedroom and said that she was taking Lily to the hospital.

"I'm fine, Aunt Dolores, just a little setback," Lily said.

"Nonsense," Aunt Dolores said. She got Lily into a sitting position, helped her dress, and then guided her down to the car.

"He doesn't know," Lily said.

"I'll tell him," Aunt Dolores said. "He has to know."

"Please don't. He'll just punish me. And his mother will punish me."

"You've done nothing wrong, Lily. Now close your eyes. Don't think or worry."

In the nest of the car she felt safe. The seats were leather and this was a relief, for certainly she was bleeding all over the place. She saw Aunt Dolores's red lipstick, and her bracelets, and her pretty pale blue coat that came to her knees, and she saw Aunt Dolores's right calf, the length of it and she thought how lovely it was to see a woman's bare leg, and she wondered if her child had been a girl. She wanted to say that she didn't want to see Dr. Giesbrecht, but she was too tired to talk, and she closed her eyes.

The doctor who performed the D&C was a woman with lots of black curly hair and a voice that rasped as she described the procedure to Lily. It was such a relief to have a woman touching her that Lily wanted to weep, but she was too tired. Aunt Dolores came to her after the procedure and said that she was going to take Lily to her house, where she would recuperate.

"But I have to make supper for Johan," Lily said. "And there are dirty dishes in the sink."

"Let him fix his own meal," Aunt Dolores said. "Or go over to his mother's. I'm sure she'd be happy to have her boy back. You're coming home with me."

At night she woke disoriented. There was a small light coming from the adjoining bathroom and the light bled into her room and revealed a large bookshelf and a television and a side table with a lamp, and Lily recognized the lamp as Marcie's and she realized that she was in Marcie's old bedroom. The comforter on top of her was clean and smelled of the outside air, and she saw that on the bedside table, beside the lamp, there was a bowl of tomato soup and beside the bowl, on a small plate, were several crackers and a pat of butter. She picked up one of the crackers and nibbled at it.

She stayed with Aunt Dolores for one week, and during that time, because she did not have a change of clothing, she began to wear Marcie's clothes. She wore jeans for the first time in her life, as well as a flannel shirt, which was something Johan might wear, but not for women. It was soft to touch, and a little small for her so that the buttons were stretched across her chest. She wore a belt with the jeans and this too was strange and foreign, for suddenly she was worldly, dressed like a man, and she was surprised to discover that these clothes meant for a man should make her feel very much like a woman. It wasn't sexual, but more like a self-consciousness, a keen awareness of how her body was shaped, and how others might see her.

One afternoon she went with Dolores to do some grocery shopping at Penner Foods. She wore her head covering, but everything else she wore was of the world: jeans, a button-down shirt, boots that were Marcie's. She sensed that folks were looking at her, and judging her, and she hid behind her aunt as they walked the aisles. She saw one of Johan's sisters, Katerina, at the far end of the pasta aisle, but it was too late to change direction and so she cast her eyes upon the floor and did not look up as she passed Katerina by. There came a hiss and several words of condemnation, but then her aunt spoke and said that Lily just wanted to be left alone. "Go back to your village," Aunt Dolores said, and she took Lily's arm and pulled her along.

In the car later, Aunt Dolores sighed and asked if Lily was okay.

"I think I should go back home," Lily said.

"Are you sure?" her aunt asked. "You know that you can choose."

The idea of choosing was foreign and made no sense to her. She wondered if Aunt Dolores was speaking in the voice of the devil, if she had been sent to tempt her. She looked at her aunt, sitting so naturally behind the wheel of her Cutlass, speaking so certainly of choosing, and she wanted to believe that this was true, that she could choose, but she was overwhelmed by the possibility that she might choose poorly.

That night she watched television with her uncle. A program about a girl growing up in the old days, on the prairies, and the hardships involved, and the family who were kind to one another, and it reminded her of her own childhood, only the girl in the television show had a very strong voice, and she went to dances and her father played the fiddle. And so, it wasn't like her life at all.

The following morning she woke to the sound of voices, and she heard Johan speaking to her Aunt Dolores. They were out on the front driveway. She watched from her upstairs window, and she saw Johan standing beside his pickup, moving his arms around, and talking. She couldn't hear what he was saying, and she wished that she might, for she had not heard anything from his mouth in a long time. And then he climbed back into his pickup and drove off. He seemed angry, but this was not new, for he had been angry in the last while, using his large body to make his points. It always frightened her, his anger, and she went out of her way to appease him. But now she could not appease him. Nor did she want to, and this frightened her, the stubbornness she was experiencing, and the taste of inevitability in her mouth.

AND SO SHE went home. And, again, the hole opened up in Lily's heart. She fed it with the books that Aunt Dolores had given her. She fed it with doubt. And she fed it with rebellion and anger. And when the hole was full, and there was nothing else to put into it, she continued to feed it, until it spilled over and infected her mind and her body. This was what selfishness felt like, she thought.

And then Johan's brother returned. In celebration, the family held a large supper and invited folks from the church. Mr. Gerbrandt slaughtered a hog, and the whole process—the sledgehammer on the hog's head, the slicing of the belly, the blood and guts, the digging of the pit, the lighting of the coals, the settling in of the hog carcass onto the hot coals—all of this was pure pleasure for those who bent to the task. Margaret chipped in with lighting the coals, and Katerina and her mother made coleslaw and baked potatoes and plum platz. Folks arrived. The air smelled of smoked meat. Wooden tables were set up outside. Leaves the colour of ripe pumpkins fell onto the tabletops and someone said that this was God's tablecloth and wasn't it beautiful. Lawn chairs were sprung. Grace was said. A song was sung. And they ate.

Lily was present, but she was like a ghost amongst the flesh and forms of real people. She ate some pork on a homemade bun, and she ate a pickle, and she found a seat on a bale of straw off to the side. Johan finally appeared, and he took some coleslaw and some raspberry Freshie and he stood in a circle of men his age and they talked about motors. And cars. Frantz, who had not wanted this party, walked around in his clumsy manner, his head bowed slightly, and nodded at the various members of the community, who treated him kindly and told him that it was an answer to prayer. He nodded.

Smiled. Ate. And then went over to Lily and introduced himself.

Because Frantz was not baptized, and therefore was not a member of the church, he was allowed to speak to her. He stood over her, and she saw that he was huge, and that he was awkward, and she wondered if it was true that he was a lover of many women, something that she had heard from the mouths of the women in church. Earlier. When she still went to church. Of course, she didn't ask him this question. She just thought it. And she thought that he was less arrogant than Johan, her husband. For when she stood, he said, "That's not necessary."

"What's not?" she asked.

"To stand. To be polite."

"I'm not being polite," she said. "I don't want a sore neck."

He said that he was pleased to meet the wife of his little brother.

She said that she was pleased to meet the prodigal son. And when she said this she was sorry, for this was insolence.

But he just smiled and said that it was a fearful thing to come home to a roast pig and smiling faces and to know that everything was expected now.

"It is," she said.

"My father wanted this."

"He loves you."

"Not sure about that. He's worried about jewels and heaven and such."

"And you?"

"Not a bit."

This was shocking for Lily. Even though she had been shunned, and even though she was angry, she still held to some of the beliefs of her youth. And one of them was heaven.

Frantz said that he was going to step away. He said that they had said enough words. And so he did exactly that, and he walked over to the food table and took another helping of pork. His sister Margaret found him and threw herself at him, holding his arm, and going up on tiptoes to say something in his ear. Frantz laughed.

Lily did not speak to him again for a month. She saw him around the farm, and she saw him leave the yard in his father's pickup, and she saw him sitting outside his shack, smoking. She waved at him. He waved back. But they did not speak at that time. This would come later, one day in the egg room. She was stacking flats when he entered. She heard him, but did not turn. He rolled his cart into the centre of the room and then trudged about heavily. She could smell feed on his overalls, and there was also a hint of coffee, which must have bled from his large mouth. Ever since the homecoming barbecue she had heard the family talking about Frantz. She heard again of his wayward ways, and heard that he had squandered whatever money he had. She knew that his return home signified something, though what it signified she could not say. She also knew that Johan resented his brother's return, for now there was another son in the family, and though Frantz might not have returned to claim anything, Johan feared that he would want a section of the farm, and he would want the egg quota, and the patriarch, Mr. Gerbrandt, who was overjoyed that his eldest son had returned, might indeed be willing to give Frantz whatever he wanted. Again, Lily gleaned much of this from watching and listening. She saw the change in Johan when Frantz was near. She saw that Johan became sullen. She heard the sisters talking. She once overheard Johan talking to his mother about how Frantz had tricks and he was still errant and how was it that their father could not see the trickery. She could have shared her views of Frantz with Johan, but Johan of course did not speak to her, and he might not have agreed with Lily's view of Frantz. Which was that Frantz was not interested in the farm, and he was not interested in the egg quota, and he was home for only a brief stay and then he would leave again. She hadn't heard this from Frantz's mouth, but she knew it as one senses frost before it arrives early, or as one knows that if you beat a dog often enough, it will learn to cower at the slightest gesture.

Frantz was ugly. This was so. It had always been so, and it still was, and it was a mystery to Lily how a man as ugly as Frantz might have managed to attract the many women he was rumoured to have seduced. She discovered, after several weeks working in the barn with Frantz—for this is where he spent his time—that she had become accustomed to his fierce looks, and so his ugliness no longer surprised her, in fact she had become more curious than repulsed by his size and his strange physical qualities. He stood over six and a half feet, and his neck was wide and short and there were times when she studied him that he appeared to have no neck at all. The overalls he wore were too small for him, and so this made him appear even larger. His feet were wide and long and once, when he had left his boots in the egg room, she had stood and looked down at them and realized that she might be able to fit both of her feet into one of them. If he had the weight and fearsomeness of a giant, his nature was that of a child. She had never seen him angry, and she had never seen him strike out in any way at anything, unlike Johan, who was impatient and, when he still spoke with her, might raise his voice if she didn't anticipate his desire for ketchup with his meatloaf, or a new bar of soap in the shower. Where Frantz was meek and soft, Johan was demanding and hard. And so she learned that meekness and kindness was also a form of seduction.

When Frantz spoke to her in the egg room, she thought that he had simply cleared his throat. But then he cleared his throat again and she realized that he was speaking to her.

"I got myself a dog," he said.

She waited, and then turned. He was standing behind his cart, looking down at her. He wore a baseball cap that said John Deere and his awesome face was spotted with stubble and his hands were folded on top of the flats on his cart and she thought that the eggs might get crushed, but all seemed fine and safe. He shuffled his feet.

"It's a Lab," he said.

"Your mother doesn't like dogs," she said. This was an accepted fact—Mrs. Gerbrandt hated dogs.

He shrugged. "I decided. The dog will sleep in my shack. I'll feed it. It's a hunting dog."

"Do you hunt?" she asked.

"I plan to."

She smiled slightly. "You'll need a gun," she said.

"I plan to get one."

"And a hunting license?"

"I plan to."

"Sounds like you have plans," she said.

He smiled. "My brother thinks I shouldn't."

"Shouldn't get a gun? Or shouldn't get a license? Or shouldn't have plans."

"All three."

"He probably didn't want you to get a dog either."

"He didn't."

"But you did."

Though he was five years older than Johan, he looked younger, and his eyes had lines at the corners that made it appear that he was constantly smiling, even when he wasn't. He liked to announce his life to folks, as he had done with the dog just now. Lily thought that he might not be as simple as he appeared, or as Johan and his family wanted him to appear.

He said that he would show her the dog.

"Not now," she said. "I have to go start supper for Johan. Maybe tomorrow."

"Johan's crazy," he said.

"Oh I don't know."

"No no, not crazy like that. He's crazy not to talk to you. Not to eat with you."

"We eat together," Lily said. She was defensive.

He agreed with her by nodding his big head. Then he turned away and left her alone.

That night she sat across from Johan and studied his face as he ate. He liked to cut the kernels off of his cob of corn, and he was doing that now, concentrating on sliding his knife down towards the plate. He bit his upper lip as he worked, as if he might be performing a very serious operation. When he was done he took a piece of butter and dropped it into the pile of corn. He looked up at her, and caught her watching. She ducked her head. She heard him eating, the corn crunching in his teeth.

She held a silent conversation in her head, for this is how she managed herself. She would tell Johan that Frantz had talked to her, and Johan would say that she shouldn't listen to anything Frantz said. She would say that Frantz was gentle and meant no harm and then she would ask why Johan hated him. I don't hate him, Johan would say, and she would answer that it seemed so, or perhaps he was jealous of his older brother. I feel nothing, Johan would say. Nothing. She would say then that Frantz had a dog and he wanted to hunt, and Johan would say that all his life Frantz has wanted. And he gets. And he gets. And she would say that Frantz thought Johan was crazy not to love her. And Johan would say that their marriage had nothing to do with Frantz. And he would tell her to stay away from his brother.

This is what she thought as they finished the meal. Her mind awhirl. She rose and collected the dirty dishes. Was she crazy? She scraped the leftovers, bones from the roast and scraps of gravy and potatoes, into a container and snapped on a lid. She set it aside by the sink. She heard Johan rise from the table. Into the foyer where he put on his boots and jacket. The door opened. The door closed. She saw him pass under the yard light and move towards his parents' house. Ever since Frantz's return, Johan visited his parents in the evening. Shared dessert with them. Drank coffee. Made sure that Frantz did not bury himself too deeply in the father's affections.

When she had finished the dishes she wiped the counter, and then picked up the container with the leftovers and she pulled on her boots and slipped into her parka and she went outside in the cold night air and she squeaked across the snow towards the shack and knocked. No answer. She knocked again, and she called out and she heard the whine of the dog. She opened the door and stepped inside. The smell of wood smoke. One room with a bed, and a little table upon which there was a lamp and few pieces of paper and a pencil and some books. The dog lay beside the stove. It rose and wagged its rump. She kneeled and put the container down and held the dog's head and said, "Hey boy. Or are you a girl? Hey. Hey. You sweet thing." The dog's tongue was wet and warm and Lily's face got a cleaning. She pulled back and picked up the container of leftovers and snapped open the lid and held it for the dog. And it was gone. The container clattered to the floor.

She sat, the floor cold beneath her legs. The dog rested its snout on her lap. She talked to the dog and asked its name and she said that it must be cold. She decided then and there that a blanket was necessary and so she rose and patted the dog on the head and promised to return. In her house she took the bathroom rug with its rubber undercoating, and she rolled it up and carried it under her arm and trudged back across the yard to the shack. She laid the rug out for the dog and settled it down and rubbed its ears and said that this would be better and warmer and now the night would not be so cold. When she left the dog an hour later, it whimpered and she said that she would come back in the morning with milk and scrambled eggs.

There were the laws of the community, and there were natural laws, and she recognized that though she might rebel against the laws of the community, she could not fight the laws of nature. She was alone, and her heart was colder now, and that coldness was simply a matter of saving herself. If she could not achieve happiness, then at least she would measure herself against the yardstick of her mind. Heart and mind. Mind and heart. She was like the dog, waiting for someone to come along and lay out a bathroom rug for warmth. And food to eat. And a voice in the ear. A pat on the head.

The following afternoon, in the egg room, she told Frantz that she had fed his dog.

"I noticed," he said.

"I gave him scrambled eggs with cheese this morning. And a piece of toast. And a bowl of milk."

"Don't let Johan see you. He'll shoot the dog."

"Or me," she said. And as soon as she said this, she was sorry. And now Frantz was looking at her.

"Does he hurt you?" Frantz asked.

"Oh, no. Not at all. That would be paying attention."

She felt that her words had betrayed Johan and she was sorry. She said that she would work now, and she left Frantz in the egg room and headed out into the barn.

The dog's name was Schlacks. Frantz had named him this because he was gangly and loose. She visited Schlacks every day after supper, when Johan went to his parents' place for dessert. One evening, while sitting with Schlacks, the door opened and she looked up and saw Frantz. He closed the door. He stood over where she was sitting on a wooden stool, brushing Schlacks. He was carrying a bowl of dessert, apple crumble with ice cream, and he handed it to her. She gave it to the dog, who ate it quickly, the bowl sliding across the floor.

"It was for you," Frantz said.

"I don't eat sweets," Lily said.

Frantz squatted beside her and lit a cigarette. She saw the shape of his hand, and the arch of his nose as the match flared. His wide unlucky mouth.

"Do you have money?" he asked.

She didn't understand the question, or the reason for the question. She wondered if he wanted her money, though she had nothing. She said that Johan kept the money and gave it to her should she need some.

"And he does?"

"If needed."

"It seems you don't need much."

She thought about this, and had no answer. She stood and said that she would go.

"Is someone calling you?"

"No. But I have dishes to wash. And Johan will wonder."

"You think so? Johan is right now sitting on his mother's lap and eating crumble while his sisters stroke his head."

"Good night," she said.

"Good night, Lily."

THAT NIGHT SHE dreamed that Frantz was kissing her knuckles with his large mouth. And she did not stop him, for she was happy. When she woke she was ashamed because she had been happy. Afraid to sleep because she might dream, she turned on the bedside lamp and she picked up a book and she read. This was a book of poetry that Aunt Dolores had delivered to her. The insistence in Dolores's voice as she said, "Here. Read this." She didn't know poetry. She didn't understand it. But the shortness of the lines. And the feelings. Feelings for no good reason. She thought that there might be rules for poetry, as there were rules for everything else. She wanted to know what the rules were, but she couldn't make sense of them. Sometimes the poems rhymed, sometimes they didn't. The poems she read were not long. They were written by a woman who was now dead. This she knew.

> Before I got my eye put out—
> I liked as well to see
> As other creatures, that have eyes—
> And know no other way—

But were it told to me, Today,
That I might have the Sky
For mine, I tell you that my Heart
Would split, for size of me—

The Meadows—mine—
The Mountains—mine—
All Forests—Stintless stars—
As much of noon, as I could take—
Between my finite eyes—

The Motions of the Dipping Birds—
The Morning's Amber Road—
For mine—to look at when I liked,
The news would strike me dead—

So safer—guess—with just my soul
Opon the window pane
Where other creatures put their eyes—
Incautious—of the Sun—

She read the poem three or four times, but did not know
what to make of it. She liked that first line. Was this her? You
could put out a fire, and you could put out a cat from the
house, and you might put out a candle. But an eye? Like a
tongue? And only one eye? What about the other eye, which
would still see? And the soul, pressed against the windowpane. And safer? Why safer? Was the soul more important
than the eyes?

She heard Johan snoring in the next room. Her eyes closed.

THIS WAS THE winter she worked for the neighbour family, Gretchen and Carlos and their three children. It had been Johan's idea, and he had done all the arranging. He came into the house one evening and he began to talk. He did not talk because there had been a thaw in their relationship, this she knew. He only talked when he had to hand out information, or when he had to give orders, and when the commandments were finished, so was his talking. On this evening, he said that Gretchen Wall was looking for someone two days a week, on Thursdays and Fridays. Gretchen was teaching a midwifery course in the city, and she needed a woman in the house to help with the children, especially the nine-month-old. The two older children were of school age, but they were home-schooled by Gretchen. This was a family that had moved to the country from the city in order to homestead. They wanted a quieter life for their children, fewer outside influences, and they wanted the experience of the countryside, of growing food, of raising sheep, of putting their hands into the soil. Lily was reminded of her own life, and how she had been raised, though the Wall children had more freedom, and they had books, and they did not have religion.

And so Lily went to work for the Walls. Their house was adjacent to the Gerbrandt yard, and it took five minutes to walk the path through the stand of poplars. The house was rundown and dirty, and there were children's toys everywhere, and there was laundry that needed ironing, and because Carlos didn't have a machine shed there were tools scattered about, and in the mud room there were animal traps for beaver and wolves and there was a roll of 22-gauge copper wire for rabbit snares. Lily knew snares. Her father had taught her as a girl.

The thing is, Carlos, the father of the children, was always around when she worked, but he was not domestic, and so it was like having one more child, and it turned out that Lily in the end was taking care of four children. She cooked lunch, and she prepared supper—sometimes chili, sometimes noodle casserole—and she tried to get the cooking done when Oscar, the nine-month-old, was down for his nap. When her hands were free. But then the older children, Astrid and Aldo, demanded attention as well, and so these were the times when she sat with them on the couch by the woodstove and read to them while Carlos strummed his guitar in the next room and smoked marijuana. At least she thought it might be marijuana. It stank like a car that has, a week earlier, hit a skunk on the road. This was different than the smell of Frantz's cigarettes. Carlos asked her one time if she partook, and she said that she wasn't allowed to smoke. He nodded and smiled. He spoke Spanish. When Gretchen came home she always spoke English with Carlos, and she spoke English with the children, and Carlos spoke Spanish with everyone, and the children responded in English, and they all understood each other.

The children were completely happy with their lives. They were fed tons of raw vegetables, which were the staples in the house, and they sat willingly at the table to do their math homework, and they had few complaints about the clothes they wore, which had been purchased at the MCC store in town, and they ate no sugar, and for fun they put on little theatre shows organized by Astrid, who was eight, and they did not do battle with each other, and sometimes, in the after-noons, as Oscar slept in his crib, the older children made art while Lily tackled the pile of laundry and Carlos strummed his guitar in the next room, and in those moments, any stranger walking in would have seen a happy family, with Lily the mother of that family.

Lily liked the sound of the guitar. In her community the only musical instrument was the voice, given by God. Lily's voice was clear and beautiful, and the first time she sang with the children it was in the living room, when Astrid had put a record on the player and the song "I'll Fly Away" was one that Lily knew. She thought she was alone with the children, and so she was loose and playful, and she was not afraid to lift her voice. When the song ended she heard someone clapping and Astrid called "Papa," and she saw Carlos standing in the doorway. He nodded and said that her voice was fine. Where did she learn to sing? In church, she said. She looked away, embarrassed. He said that church was good for something then.

The following week Carlos showed her three chords on the guitar: C, G, and F.

He taught her how to strum, using a pick. She was clumsy at first and he had to place her fingers on the frets, using his own rough hands, and she was aware of him touching her, and she was aware of his chest against her shoulder. He said, "There," and then he said "Good," and then he took the guitar from her and began a song that she knew, "Farther Along," and she sang softly along with him. His English was very good when he sang, not so good when he spoke. This was curious.

One afternoon she baked oatmeal cookies with the children as Oscar slept. Astrid played some rock and roll on the stereo and the children danced in the living room. The world in this house was so different, so strange, so contrary. Lily's heart was big at that moment. The children wanted her to dance with them. She said that she didn't know how to dance. Astrid cried, "Lily, we'll show you." And she dragged her out into the middle of the living room, and against her own will, but for the sake of the children, Lily moved her feet slowly and maybe even snapped her fingers slightly. The song was inside her, and it was outside her, and it was around her. They were dancing like this when Gretchen came home. She dropped her bag at the door and joined them. She held Lily's hands and closed her eyes and mouthed the words. The kids screamed. They loved it when their mother danced. Lily was in a maelstrom. This was not her life. She stepped back and watched the children and their mother dance. She went to find Oscar, who was standing in his crib, shaking the side, wanting freedom. She picked him up and laid him on the change table and changed his diaper. He kicked his fat legs. She smelled his head. Picked him up. In the living room, when he saw his mother dancing, his feet thumped and he began to cry and Gretchen came to him and took him and sat and opened her blouse and gave him her breast. Gretchen's other breast was bared as well because Oscar like to play with the free nipple as he fed. Lily went into the kitchen to stack the cookies. When she was finished she put on her coat and peeked into the living room to say goodbye. The older children flanked their mother now, who had closed her blouse, and Oscar sat on her lap. Milk ran down his chin.

Gretchen said that she had planned to pay her. She should look in the purse, in the wallet for the money. She told her what to take, and Lily did as directed. She slipped the money into her jacket pocket. She said goodbye and stepped outside and as she walked the path through the poplars she ran into Carlos, who was heading home, a rabbit in his right hand.

"Supper," Carlos said, and he held up the rabbit for her to see. He always looked her in the eyes when he talked to her, and she was always aware of the blackness of his eyes, and she was aware of his intensity, and how he didn't look away. And so she looked away. And when she looked back, he was still looking at her.

"Goodbye," she said, and she passed him by.

At home, she put the money on the kitchen counter. It wasn't her money. It was the household's.

THIS WAS THE same winter that she stopped wearing her head covering. And when she was alone in the house she wore jeans underneath her dress during the day, just to see. She removed the jeans before Johan came in for lunch and supper. One time she took a dark pencil crayon and wet the tip under the tap and touched the colour to her eyelids and lashes. She spent an hour in front of the mirror, experimenting, washing away her efforts and then reapplying the pencil crayon. She left the crayon on for lunch, to see if Johan would notice. He did not. He concentrated on eating his soup and bread, and then he left. Another time she unpinned her hair and let it fall to her waist, and when she cleaned the toilet and washed the kitchen floor her hair was everywhere and wild and she felt loose and wanton. She wore her hair in that manner throughout the morning and then pinned it up before lunch, even though there was no expectation that Johan would notice or say anything. One night, going to bed, she found her head covering lying on her pillow and she realized that Johan had put it there for her to find.

This was also the winter that Aunt Dolores spent time with her. Every Tuesday, Dolores picked her up at nine o'clock and together they drove the roads that cross-hatched the countryside and they talked, and often they ended up at a small restaurant in a small town where they ate lunch together. Dolores always paid, for it was a fact that Lily had no money. Aunt Dolores wore a mink coat and she wore pink leather gloves and her hair was always perfect and she wore pumps and stockings and around her neck was a string of pearls. Unlike Lily's mother, and Johan's mother, Dolores did not purse her lips when she heard of some sin that had been committed. In fact, it was immediately clear that Aunt Dolores did not believe in sin. Or if she did, she dismissed the judgement of that sin. And because of this, it was easy to speak to Dolores of doubt and God and clothes and rules and sex. There was no subject that was verboten or out of bounds.

One day, at lunch in Landmark, in a tiny restaurant where they shared a bowl of vegetable soup and a ham sandwich, Dolores said that she had, after the birth of her final child, suffered deeply. "So lost I was that I wandered around the house calling out 'What should I do? What should I do?' I ended up in Winkler, in the hospital there. This was a necessary move, but horrible. We were expected to play games, and we were expected to do crafts, which I hated. Popsicle sticks and white glue that stuck to my fingers. And so one day I refused, and everyone was upset. The nurses especially. Nurses like order. They like to be obeyed. And I didn't obey. And so I was relegated to my room during craft hour as a form of punishment. Only it wasn't a punishment. I was finally alone. I could sit on my chair and look out the window at the rabbits hopping through the snow. I loved the sight of those rabbits going going. Where were they going, I wondered. And in the afternoon I was taken for my shock therapy and I promptly forgot everything in my life. I forgot the names of my children. I forgot that my husband, your Uncle Henry, liked butter rather than margarine, or that he liked his eggs over easy. For six weeks, this was my life." She stopped talking. Smiled. "But now I am here. And I recall the names of my children. And I know about butter. And I know about over easy. How about you, Lily? Do you have someone to talk to?"

"You, Aunt Dolores. And I work for Carlos and Gretchen. They talk to me. And their children. And I talk to Frantz." Lily shrugged. "Frantz thinks that Johan is crazy to ignore me."

"Of course he is. Absolutely. Throwing away a beautiful wife. But then, he is ruled by rules, and he is ruled by the church, and he is ruled by his family. First his family."

"Do you think so?"

"Yes. I know this. I can see this. His mother is very fearful. Always has been. She wouldn't let her little boy get away with anything. I'm surprised she allowed him to marry you."

"Oh, I was different then. They didn't know what they were getting."

Dolores laughed. "Oh Lily," she said. She dabbed at her mouth with a napkin and then twisted her pearls. "Marcie asks about you," she said.

"Does she?" Marcie was travelling and working in Holland for the year and Lily missed her.

"Of course. I don't know why she went to that country. She gets terribly homesick. She calls me and cries horribly and then she goes away happy and rides her bicycle to the bakery and she leaves me with her sadness."

Lily was quiet. Then she said, "Marcie's lucky. To have you as a mother."

"Oh, I don't think so. I'm not a good mother." Then she said, "We have to help you."

Lily was surprised. "How? And why?"

"You're stuck."

"Oh, I'm not stuck."

"You wouldn't know if you were stuck, would you? Is Frantz making eyes at you?"

Lily blushed. Shook her head.

"And you wouldn't know that either, would you? He's a single man. He might be ugly, but he's a sweet talker."

"He's not very handsome, that's true."

"That's kind of you. The fact is he's ugly. Poor fellow."

"His heart is beautiful. And his words."

Dolores smiled. "It's a dangerous thing to shun a girl like you. Stop talking to Lily, lock her away, and she'd end up thinking the neighbour's cow was worth bedding."

"Auntie."

"You should want to have sex. It's only normal."

"Oh, I want to." She said this so emphatically that she was embarrassed.

But Dolores didn't seem to notice. She said, "I used to like it. Very much. And then I had that therapy, and now I'm on pills, and everything's shifted. My world has shifted considerably." She sighed. "Poor Henry."

"He took me shopping," Lily said. "Frantz." She ducked her head and then looked up to see if her aunt was surprised or shocked. Dolores was sipping at her coffee and waiting.

Lily said that Frantz had taken her into town for some milk and butter and flour, and on the way home he'd stopped at Reidiger Clothing and they'd gone in together where he'd picked up a shirt and socks and while in the store he'd suggested that she might need something for herself. He would pay. And he insisted she try on a pair of jeans, and she had done so, had even come out of the change room and showed them to him while the salesgirl watched, which was strange because it felt like the girl was watching her and judging her. Frantz said that the jeans were perfect. But she didn't know where or when she'd ever wear them, and he said that she would wear them. For sure. And so he bought them for her, and he bought a short-sleeved blouse for her that was a solid black colour. "It's quite short, the blouse, and if I lift my arms my belly button shows. I have no reason to wear it. It mostly sits in my drawer. Along with the jeans. Though sometimes I wear them in the house, under my dress."

"Frantz should know better. He's using you to get at his brother. That's what's wrong here. You didn't do anything, Lily. You have to stop being so frightened. You have your own mind. Your own body. It's no one else's. You know that, don't you?"

"I think so."

"Those brothers," Dolores said. "I'll have a talk with Frantz."

"Oh no. Don't. He hasn't done anything."

"Still. Listen. If he tries any tricks, you let me know. Okay?"

To this she had no answer.

IN THE MORNING, standing at the sink washing dishes, she saw a bird fly directly into the windowpane and disappear. She was shaken, for it was a large bird, and it made a thud and there was a smear of blood on the pane where the bird had hit. She leaned forward to see if the bird was lying on the ground. It was. Black against the white snow. She watched the bird struggle for breath, and then it stopped struggling. And died. Certainly a broken neck.

She missed sex. She missed the anticipation as much as the act itself, in fact it had always been that way. That the thought of sex was more fun than lying down and doing it. She found herself thinking about others and how they had sex and if they had sex and if so how often. She imagined that Mrs. Gerbrandt had sex with Mr. Gerbrandt, simply because Mr. Gerbrandt was highly sexed, and she knew this because he had said a few things to her in private, odd things, about her hair, and about her looks, or how the dress she wore looked on her, and one time he had touched her back while passing her by, for no necessary reason, and she knew that he wasn't stopping himself from falling, he was a strong capable man, and it doesn't take much as a young woman to know when you are being touched in a certain way. She didn't give it much thought back then, and it didn't worry her, for Mr. Gerbrandt was clean as a whistle, or sort of clean with maybe a bit of spittle in the whistle, but still, she was off limits. This she knew. And she wondered if Mrs. Gerbrandt had touched Mr. Gerbrandt's penis, or if he asked her to, and with that same thought came the thought of Frantz and she wondered how many women had touched him down there. And had they touched him with their mouths, or just their hands?

The slide towards Frantz took place over the winter, specifically on Sunday mornings when the family was at church, and Lily and Frantz were left alone. They worked together in the barn, gathering eggs. They spoke in the refrigerator room, sorting the eggs. One morning he made her coffee and brought it to her. She took it from his hands. She said thank you. She asked if he had eaten breakfast. He hadn't. She said that she would prepare him something. She left to go back to her house and he appeared half an hour later and sat at her table while she served him toast and eggs and fried potatoes. They were both aware of the clock, and they were aware when the family would return, and so they were in cahoots. Though they did not talk of it. She sat across from him and watched him eat. He was more delicate than Johan, who held his fork as if it were a shovel, and used his left thumb to push the food onto the shovel. Frantz ate slowly, and he talked as he ate, so much that she worried his food might be getting cold. But he didn't seem concerned about this.

At first he didn't seem curious about her. He talked about himself, about his travels and the various jobs he'd had after he'd left home, some of them back-breaking and some of them easy. He had for a time travelled in Central America, where he'd lived in a small coastal town on the Pacific side and learned to surf and spent his days languishing. He said the word languishing and he laughed, as if it went against every tenet he'd been raised with. He said that there was a whole wide world out there that his people were afraid of. That she might be afraid of. He lifted his head and looked at her and smiled.

She said that she wasn't afraid of what was out there. She said that he was single. He was free to do as he wished.

"You're free," he said. "Look at you. I don't know another girl like you." He cleaned his plate and said that she was a good cook.

"Just eggs," she said. "Nothing special."

Then, as if this was a continuation of some other conversation, she said that she often read things that she didn't understand. "Or I think I understand, but I wonder if I'm missing something."

"You're smart enough," he said. "Truth is, stupid people don't get shunned."

She smiled again. "I don't think we should talk about this," she said. "It's wrong."

"That's exactly what they want you to believe. They want you to accept. They want you to not think. To not ask questions. To be humble."

"Humility is a good thing."

"Is it? Are they humble? Is Johan humble?"

"He's trying his best."

"Are you happy?" he asked.

She said even if she wasn't happy now, at this moment, she thought that she might be happy again. Soon.

"I told Johan that he would lose you."

"You shouldn't have said that. It isn't true."

On that day—this was before everything that followed—he stood and carried his plate to the sink, and as he passed her by he placed his free hand on her shoulder and held it there for a moment, and so this was the first time he touched her. She was aware of the touch, and how it was a message, though she did not know if it was a message of consideration, or pity, or seduction. In their world, the touch would have been considered a form of theft. She saw herself as an empty house, with a locked door, and she wondered if Frantz might be waiting for the key to open that door.

Over the next while, in the egg room together, or simply standing in the yard, their breath pluming into the cold air, they argued about God. And doubt. And right and wrong. He was scornful of everything they had been taught. Not in a mocking manner, and not to upset her, but he just didn't believe, and she couldn't believe how it was possible not to believe. She felt sorry for him. And wished him a clear head. And a clear heart. So that he might believe again.

Two weeks later, on a Sunday morning, in the egg room, he told her of a trip he had taken down to Central America, and

of the people he had spent time with. He spoke of a woman
he had met, and he said her name, Annalee. He said they had
travelled to a place called Santiago, and in the market he had
seen a man preaching. The man was dressed in a suit, and he
held a Bible, and he had a beautiful voice. Frantz said that the
man turned in a slow circle as he spoke. He said that there
were two boys with the man, his sons certainly, and they were
about eight and ten. The boys were dressed in suits as well,
and they stood at the man's side, and as the man turned, so
did the boys. Sometimes the boys looked up at the man, and
then looked down at their feet, and then looked at each other
and nudged each other and smiled. As if they had a secret. Or
as if they were relieved to have one other person share their
shame. For they must have felt shame. There they were, standing in the market while their father called out the sins of the
world and the path to redemption as the indifferent crowds
flowed past. "I saw myself," Frantz said. "And I saw my life. I
recalled going to town with my parents and my brother and
my younger sisters, and I recalled being seen in a certain
manner, and I recalled the looks strangers gave us. We had
been taught, not through words, but through actions and
comportment, to be proud of who we were. It was a form of
pride. We were better than other people. Except that I knew
that this was not true. I knew that we were just odd and I
didn't want to be odd. I wanted to go unnoticed. And when I
saw those boys, I saw myself, and I saw how I would have
been seen by strangers. I tried to explain this to Annalee, the
woman I was with, but she didn't get it. She thought the boys
were cute. She said that the boys seemed happy. She saw the
preacher, and she saw the boys, and she saw what might be
called a carnival. A circus act. A barker in a travelling show. I

saw something very different. I saw the triviality of my ances-
tors. The insignificance of myself. I saw obscurity."

He stopped talking. And then he said that he had not meant
to give her some strange confession.

Lily's feet could not move. All that Frantz had said was
true. The story he had told was her story, even though his
story was more exotic, and hers was dull. She had not been in
a market. And she had not been with a lover. And she had not
been far from home. Still.

She said, "I understand. Your story. What you felt. I understand. The insignificance."

"Of course you do," he said.

She stepped towards him and took his face in her hands
and she touched his eyes and his mouth and his jaw and his
nose. She touched his neck and his ears and she felt stubble
on his chin. She had to reach up to touch him, for he was tall.
What was surprising to her was his effort to help her. He
crouched slightly and bent towards her and the whole time
she was touching him he kept his eyes open and looked at her.
They said nothing the rest of that morning. They worked side
by side, and they stacked the flats of eggs, and at noon they
went to their separate houses.

That day, for supper, she made a rice casserole for Johan,
and she served it with canned corn and a Jell-O salad. A bowl
of ice cream for dessert. She made coffee and poured it for
Johan, and in the silence she heard the movement of his
tongue around the ice cream.

She took a pen and a piece of paper and she wrote on the
paper: I need money.

Johan wrote back: Why?

For tampons, she wrote. And underwear. She wrote: Now.

He stood and left the room and returned with a ten-dollar bill and placed it in front of her.

She wrote: I want money each week. Enough for me to buy my necessities.

He wrote: Ask me when you need it and we'll see.

She wrote: It's our money.

He wrote: You have no money.

To this she had no response. For it was true. She had nothing.

She stood and cleared the dishes. She ran hot water in the sink and buried the dirty dishes in the water and she put on her rubber gloves and she washed the dishes and the cutlery and the glasses. She scrubbed the Corning Ware of the food that was stuck, and then she removed her rubber gloves and she dried the dishes.

That night, after Johan was sleeping and snoring, she rose and dressed and went downstairs on tiptoes and put on her parka and boots and stepped outside and felt the cold air on her bare head and she walked across the snow and knocked on his door.

HE WANTED TO touch her and he asked if he could and when at first she said no, he said that he understood. She said that she shouldn't have touched him as she did in the egg room. But she had been curious and she had been impulsive. She was sorry. Two weeks after that, on a Thursday night, at three-thirty in the morning, she removed her clothes and lay down beside him.

And they talked. And talked. And it was everything to her. She wondered sometimes if she didn't visit him simply to hear his voice. When Frantz spoke to Lily, she spoke back. When she spoke back, they became conversant. When they became conversant, they spoke more intimately. When they spoke in this manner, intimately, she approached him as a possibility. And he saw the possibility in her. He spoke. She spoke. They spoke. They pushed each other away, and fell back together, like a bottle tossed against the shore and then pushed out again, and then back against the rocks.

One time they spoke of God and faith and her shame for having slipped away from the church. But when he asked if it was true that she felt shame, and would she go back to the church, she said no, she wouldn't. And so the shame was made up, or convenient, or necessary. He said this, and she thought about it. She said that she didn't know where his ideas came from. So contradictory. So different. Not normal, she said.

"Oh, no," he said. "You've become so accustomed to abnormal thinking that you don't know when thinking is clear and strong and good. For example, you are burning for something else."

"What else?"

"Words. Real words. Ideas. The church you and I grew up in is bereft of ideas. In fact, they are afraid of ideas, because ideas might sow doubt, and doubt is dangerous. They want certainty."

One time they spoke of dancing. He had learned to dance in Nicaragua, on the beach where parties went all night. "At first I was embarrassed. Self-conscious. And when you dance, you can't be self-conscious. It is like making love. It is better to not think. To feel is good. That is dancing."

She said that she had danced with the children at Gretchen's. The family had taught her. And so she was now like him.

Except that she hadn't danced on a beach. "Did you dance with girls?" she asked.

He laughed and said yes, of course. And boys. And older women. And men.

She asked him how many girls he'd had. She wanted to know. He said that a number meant nothing, though there were a few, but those girls had offered him little clarity in his life, not that he'd been looking for clarity, ha, but now he was clearer. He was finding himself now. She said that she had not yet found herself. She didn't know if it was possible. She said that sometimes she caught herself standing in one place, and she realized that she had been standing there for a long time, for her feet were cold, and her face, and time had passed and she had forgotten what direction she was going in. She said that other times she was aware of moving physically through her house, but she was standing above herself, and she was watching herself, and it was odd to watch from above. In those moments it was as if she had passed from here to there, and her soul was above her body. One time when this happened she was acutely aware of the shape of her head, and she could see her mouth moving, and Johan was there, but he wasn't paying attention.

They spoke of an afterlife. She believed in one. He didn't.

He said that she just had to say the word and he would go away with her. "You wouldn't even have to take anything, just yourself."

"I couldn't," she said. "I can't."

She was shaking. He said that she could do whatever she liked. He had no possession of her. It was just an offer.

"I'd lose everything," she said.

He asked her what she had now and she had no answer.

In the morning, she was aware of her hands plucking eggs from the troughs in the barn, and she was aware of her breathing, and she was aware of her forearms in the cooler, the down of her hair and her small wrists. She felt bad for wanting sex. She had felt the same way with Johan, guilty for making sex important. And then it had stopped with Johan, and she missed it terribly.

Always, when she visited him she wore jeans and a blouse, clothes that they had bought together that day in town. And she'd known then that the secrecy of that moment in the shop was a giant step into a quagmire that might sink her. But she didn't care. Or perhaps she cared too much. And so it came to be that when she visited him in the night, she wore the blouse and the jeans and she loved the way the clothes held her, and she loved the act of removing the clothes, the jeans especially, the rushed pulling of the legs downwards so that they inevitably came off inside out and had to be turned aright later, and the bone-coloured buttons on the blouse, buttons that were delicate and small and required extra care, and it was difficult with shaking hands, for her hands often shook in those moments, and she didn't know if it was excitement or fear.

"Look at your little hands," Frantz said, and he took them and held them and then he covered her with his body. Wild, she was. She frightened herself so. But he kept opening the door. Come in. Come in. Come in. And so she did come in.

The body of course was an envelope that held the soul, which is what she had been taught from an early age, and it was crucial to not adorn or love the envelope too much, but now she saw that this was simply a lie, and she used Frantz as a test, to see if there were limits. One time as he read to her—

he was insisting on reading a book she had never heard of and found frightening for its story of jealousy—she listened and then told him to stop. Enough, she said. She was naked, and she stood and kissed him on the mouth and she walked around his room, touching the objects on his desk, and at his small table. Then she paused before him and asked him to touch her and to name the parts that he touched. To use words. Vulgar words. Real body words. He did this. And touched her as he did so. And she was thrilled by the combination of the words and his touch.

She dreamed of being consumed by a fire at night. She dreamed of dying in a snowstorm. She dreamed of drowning. She woke from these dreams, gasping, ecstatic to be alive. She thought of the movement of time, and she thought of contingency, for this is a word she had come to know recently.

She sang to herself when making Johan's supper. Her step was light, her face shone.

Johan must have noticed, but he said nothing. Did nothing. Dolores noticed. On one of their Tuesday mornings, driving to Winnipeg on this day to have lunch, she asked Lily if she was pregnant.

"Oh, no." Lily laughed. "How could I be?"

"You have that glow. I know it. Something else is making you happy."

Lily said that this was true.

"It's better then, with Johan?"

"No. Not Johan." She said that it was Frantz. And she didn't know what to do about it.

"Oh, Lily. Oh," she said. "This is what happens. And you love him, this big man?"

"I do. But I love Johan too. But Johan is gone."

Dolores said that love was a strange thing. It didn't follow the rules. She asked if she and Frantz were having sex.

Lily said that the most amazing thing about her, Dolores, was that she didn't beat around the bush. "You just spit it out, and then we have to look at it. The spit."

"The problem with growing up in your world, Lily, is that you've had to learn to lie, and you've had to learn to hide things, and there's this dirty pleasure you get from lying and hiding things. And you don't even know that it's coming around to hit you on the back of the head. That's the problem with religion and rules. They lead to moral clumsiness. You might as well pack your bags and run off with ugly Frantz."

"Oh, I couldn't Aunt Dolores. Johan, everyone, would be devastated. And he's not ugly. I don't see that anymore."

"Oh, Lily, you think Johan doesn't know? You think he's stupid? You be careful. I'm worried for you."

Lily smiled sleepily, for the conversation, the ease, the heat in the car, these were all comforting. She felt better now that she had confessed.

"You should tell him. It's not too late."

"Johan? Never. He'd kill me."

"Don't. Don't say that."

"You're right. It's not true."

On this day they went to the Pancake House where Lily ordered waffles with white sauce. The waitress didn't know white sauce, and Lily wondered how it was possible that she didn't know about white sauce and waffles.

"The world is not what you think it is," Dolores said.

Lily said that Frantz was teaching her about the world. She said this bluntly. Why wouldn't he? He knew the world. She was learning. She said that there were only two people who spoke to her, "You and Frantz. And I love you both."

Dolores was nibbling at a grilled cinnamon bun. "Once on the lips, twice on the hips," she said. "Your uncle likes me to be thin."

"You *are* thin, Aunt Dolores," Lily said. "Johan liked me thin as well. Frantz likes meat. This is what he says. And I believe that all of his girlfriends were fat." She said that in order to remain safe, both from herself and from others, she imagined two Lilys. And she watched them. "Oh, there's Lily walking across the yard. Oh, there's Lily tucking into farmer sausage. And there she is putting on jeans. And oh, there's Lily lying to Johan. And Lily talking with Frantz. And Lily with her long hair down and her shoulders bare. And I see it all from above like I was Jesus, and I forgive Lily. I do."

AND THEN ONE NIGHT, after she had returned from Frantz's shack, creeping into bed, shivering from the outside air, Johan came into her room and stood in the dark and looked down on her. She saw his shadow and his shape. She heard his breathing. He said nothing. She was frightened and so said nothing as well.

At breakfast he did not look at her. He ate and wiped the egg yolk from his plate with a loose piece of her homemade bread and he stuffed it into his mouth and finished his coffee and pushed away and left. At lunch he repeated the same actions: sit down, eat, leave. And again at supper, so that she was like a keeper of some sorts, feeding a wild animal.

The following night she heard him standing outside her door, only this time he did not enter. She heard a whisper of something, and then he was gone. In the morning she saw

204 · DAVID BERGEN

five dollars lying on the floor. He had pushed it under the door. He always came to find her after she had been with Frantz. And always there would be money on the floor the following morning. Sometimes a few dollars, other times more. One time, a fifty-dollar bill.

Another woman might have burned the money. She kept it. She put it away, and within several months she had a fair amount of cash in her little box, a box that she stored under her bed. She did not say anything to Frantz, whom she still ran to in the evenings, across the white snow. He asked her if everything was okay, and she said that she was confused and tired and she didn't know anymore. She cried a little. He made her tea. She drank it. And then left him. She could not tell Frantz about the money. Why would she tell anyone? It would only be shameful. Though on a Tuesday while having coffee with Dolores she said that she knew a woman in the church—she couldn't say her name—whose husband paid her to have sex with another man. As if it made him stronger and her weaker. "This girl thinks that money and sex go hand in hand. That sex produces profit. And so sex is valuable, but at the same time it becomes less valuable. That's what Caroline said. Oh. I shouldn't have said her name."

"I didn't hear it," Dolores said. And she asked if this Caroline was in danger.

"Oh no. No danger. No. I don't think so. The money is strange though. Like a message."

"Of course it's a message. This Caroline doesn't have her own money?"

"A little. Not much. She's accruing some."

"The money from her husband."

"Yes."

"She doesn't work?"

"She works with the layers, she gathers eggs, she mucks out the barn, she makes three meals a day, but that's not for money."

Dolores was quiet, and then she said that she would be going away for a few weeks. "My head is confused, my chest is heavy, and the doctor feels I could use some help."

"Will you have visitors?"

"Henry will come."

"How do you know? I mean. How do you know you should go there? To that place?"

"Ha, well, you just know. You're underground. The world is dark. You're sad all the time. That's how."

"I'm not sad all the time."

"Of course you're not."

"Just sometimes."

"Yes. I know." Dolores said that their house was always open. "You can come live with us."

Lily said that she would wait. She was waiting for something, but didn't know what it was.

THE ELDERS CALLED a meeting with Lily. She refused to go. It was Mr. Gerbrandt who told her about the meeting, and it was to Mr. Gerbrandt that she said no. She felt sorry for him. No one had ever said no to him before, except perhaps Frantz, and now here was Lily saying an outright no.

"It is for your marriage," Mr. Gerbrandt said. "Think of Johan."

"I do think of him. I miss him."

"Come back then. Come back to the Church."

She shook her head. She said that the Church and her marriage were two different things. People were confusing what was real with what was made up. "My marriage is real. The Church is made up."

"That is blasphemy."

"No, it's true. If the Church cared so much, it wouldn't come between a husband and a wife."

"Are you coming between the husband and the wife? Is Frantz coming between the marriage?"

She bowed her head. She said that Frantz was Frantz. She said that now that she was shunned, the elders had no power over her. There would be no meeting.

Even so, the following evening there was a knock at the door, and when she opened it, four of the men from the church were standing before her, along with Mr. Gerbrandt. They entered the house and sat at the table and she served them tea. And even as she poured the tea and laid the cups in front of them, she was aware of the absurdity of her gracious-ness, and her hospitality. It was as if she could not stop herself. Just as she could not stop herself from running to Frantz in the middle of the night. She was out of control. She thought they should know this, and so she told them. She said, "I am a lost cause. Whatever you say won't help. I am impulsive, and my heart has slipped to the lowest depths. I am Lot's wife. You might as well drink your tea and go."

Mr. Gerbrandt told her to stop. He said that she was digging herself a path to hell.

"I don't care," Lily said. "I know that I should care, but I don't."

The youngest man, the one with the pink lips, the one who had had the final word the last time she had been paid a visit, said that she was loved, and there was always forgiveness for those who were loved. "We love you, Lily," he said.

She looked at this young man with his pink lips and she knew that he believed what he said, and she was moved. She said, "Thank you for telling me this. I will consider your love." She smiled at him, and he bowed his head.

She realized that he found her attractive. That her energy, her nature, was compelling him to look at her in a new way. How strange to confuse moral judgement with sexual attraction. She told the men that they were perplexed in their hearts. She said, "You are afraid of my behaviour because my actions and my words lay bare your secret thoughts. I tell the truth. You hide truth from yourselves. This frightens you."

They didn't listen. They waited for her to finish and then one of the older men read a passage from the Bible, and another man prayed, and then Mr. Gerbrandt prayed, and then the men left, and all that remained were the half-empty teacups on the table.

AND THEN ONE day she cut off her hair, hair that she had had since her birth. She took scissors from the cutlery drawer and she stood before the bathroom mirror and she held her hair with her left hand and with her right hand she began to cut. She chopped away for a long time, for there was an abundance of hair, and when she was done, the hair was lying on the linoleum, which was the same colour as her hair. She gathered it up and put it in a plastic bag and the next day she burned it in the fireplace. Now when she saw herself in the bathroom mirror, for this was the only mirror in the house, she had to look twice to know that this was Lily, for her head looked smaller, and she thought she looked like a child. She had always worn her hair pinned back, but now that she no longer had an abundance of hair behind her head, her face seemed more prominent, and her ears more conspicuous, even though there were shags of hair covering her ears. She saw her eyes and her jaw and she turned sideways to study her profile, but this was difficult because she had to twist her eyes sideways as well, and she saw mostly her nose and her mouth and her forehead. Her long hair had been pure adornment, even when pulled up into a bun, and it had been all a piece, very important, a cross between vanity and modesty, with vanity winning out, as if to say: I have the most beautiful hair in the world, but I'm not going to show you. She was more aware of her mouth now, and she made faces at herself, and she pouted, and she thought that she might ask Aunt Dolores for some lipstick, light coloured, so as not to alarm herself or anyone else. Johan surely noticed her short hair, but he said nothing. That night, he came into her room and she wondered what he would want, but he only held her head and he ran his fingers over her skull. Then he lay on his back and looked at the ceiling and he cried, something that she'd not seen him do ever. Cry.

She said that it was okay, it was just her hair, and it was not as if she had cut off her head. She laughed then because he took everything so seriously and she sat up on the side of the bed and looked down at him. Did she hate him? She didn't think so.

Frantz was confused, and he said it was the saddest thing. She said that no, it wasn't sad. It was necessary. And so he said fine fine, it is your hair, and she said yes, it is mine. He said that she looked like a boy now, and it was strange to observe her head. She did not tell him that Johan had cried over her head the night before.

Gretchen, when she saw Lily's short hair, said that she loved it, so young she looked now, and she touched her head and said that she would fix the rough edges. And so Lily sat in Gretchen and Carlos's kitchen, on a stool, and let Gretchen fix up the edges around the ears and at the back of the neck. Gretchen held up a mirror for her and Lily studied herself and said that it was all good. Carlos was present as well, hovering in the background, singing a tune, sweeping up the hair and remarking on its colour, to which Gretchen responded with a look of exasperation.

The next day, out in the yard, Carlos met her and pointed at her hair and said that it was as if she had changed one pair of boots for another, or something to that effect. This was in the yard, near the barn, when he handed her a poem written on a piece of paper, a poem that he had translated, he said, and she took it and she wondered if all men were the same, that they saw in a woman something to be taken, or they imagined that words were a form of invitation. She was not afraid of him though, even when he noticed her short hair and said that he liked it, for now he could see her ears and her jaw. My head is smaller, she said, and for some reason she removed her hat to show him. He smiled and said that her head was the perfect size. She put her hat back on and wondered once again if she had been flirting with Carlos. He had a strong face, and he was better looking than Johan, and inevitably more handsome than Frantz, but more than his good looks, his nature was soft and pliable and she wasn't sure if this was because he spoke English like a child, and therefore she might be deceived by his nature, or if she felt safe because there was Gretchen, his wife, who lived with him and kept him.

LATER THAT WEEK, in the evening, she dressed quietly and slipped out of the house and crept across the yard to his shack. She entered without knocking. The room had been cleared out. His books, his clothes, his bedding, all was gone. The dog was gone as well. She sat on the edge of the mattress and looked for a note. There was nothing. She thought that she might faint. She lay back on the mattress and she smelled his smell.

She thought that he wouldn't leave without saying goodbye, and she realized that if he had left a note, his mother might have found it, or Johan, or the sisters, and they would have destroyed it.

HE WOULD CONTACT HER, she was certain, and when two weeks had passed, and she had not heard from him, she thought he was dead. And then she heard from one of the girls that Frantz had gone back to South America, where he had a wife and a child. This was Margaret, who was not supposed to talk to Lily, but did anyway, because she was full of spite and gossip and she knew that Lily would suffer and it gave Margaret pleasure to see Lily suffer. When Margaret said this, Lily laughed and said, "You don't know what you're talking about."

Margaret shrugged. She tossed her head. She said that it was a surprise to all, but it was true. Her brother was lost, but they were praying for him. "He won't come back. My mother won't allow it."

At supper Lily watched carefully to see if Johan would look at her, or indicate some smugness, but he just ate and pushed back from the table and went upstairs. That night she heard him moving about, to the bathroom and back again. When she no longer heard him, and thought he must be sleeping, she packed a bag, a small suitcase. She lay on the bed, fully clothed, and she waited. She sat up at one point and almost stood, but then she fell back against the bed. When she opened her eyes it was much later, and she knew that she had slept. She stood and took her bag and in the dark she crept downstairs and put on her coat and gloves and a hat and picked up her bag and stepped outside. She walked up the driveway to the main road and she turned west. A car passed her and perhaps because she did not put out a hand, it did not stop. A north wind blew and it was remorselessly cold. She decided that she would have to be more forthright, and so when she saw headlights coming towards her she moved close to the pavement and she pushed out her hand and she waved. It was a pickup. It blew past her and she lowered her hand. The brake lights on the pickup came on and the truck pulled over and then the reverse lights and the pickup was coming back for her. She panicked. She could still run. But she didn't. The pickup stopped, the passenger side window went down and a voice told her to get in. She did. She placed the suitcase at her feet, closed the door, and felt the heat in the cab.

It was a young man, Clive was his name, and he came from Tourond. He worked at the window factory as a mechanic, and he'd been called in to fix a machine. "I love the nights there," he said, "All the machines standing still and waiting." He asked her name. She told him. He asked her where she was going. She said the city.

"Long trip," he said. "Especially at night. You could freeze to death."

"I won't," she said.

He was quiet for a time. Then he said, "You have a plane to catch?"

"No."

"Someone to see?"

"No someone."

He nodded. She saw only half of his face, but it seemed pleasant. Clean-shaven. A baseball cap. A nice jaw. He said that he wasn't going to the city. And he couldn't leave her out in the cold. He asked if she wanted to come to his place till morning, and then she could continue her trip. Or he or his wife would drive her to the city. He said that his wife would have no problem with this.

"You live with her?"

"I do." He smiled. "She's my wife."

"I couldn't intrude."

"No intrusion."

And then she asked him if he was safe.

He laughed. And then stopped. "Sorry," he said. "It's a strange question. Yeah, I'm safe. My wife is too. But it's up to you."

The moon was full. The fields were white. She saw a deer, and then it was gone.

"Are you running away?" he asked.

She did not answer.

"None of my business," he said.

She saw a yard light in the distance and he aimed for it. He turned off the highway and onto a driveway that led to a farm. All was quiet. Dark, save for the yard light. He climbed from the pickup and she followed. And then there was a dog, and it ran at her and she stood unmoving and waited to be bitten or eaten. The dog jumped on her and licked at her face, for it was a big dog, and she said, "Hey sweetheart, aren't you beautiful."

Clive called out and the dog retreated. "Don't be afraid," Clive said. The dog howled some and ran circles as they advanced.

The house was quiet when they entered. The dog was kept outside. It was almost morning.

His full name was Clive Letkeman and he lived with his wife Joy. He looked to be Johan's age, though he had more energy, and his eyes were sharper. Perhaps his wife kept him sharp. In the bright light of the kitchen he boiled water and steeped tea and he plugged in a space heater and pointed it at Lily, who was shivering. He brought her a blanket and handed it to her.

"Thank you," she said.

And then she told him how she lived, and she told him about her husband, and her husband's parents, and the sisters-in-law, and she said that they had layers, and as she talked she thought that anyone listening to her story would believe that her life was a fine one. Though of course Clive didn't believe her. She didn't believe herself. For what was she doing out on the highway hitchhiking if everything was fine and good?

"You'll want to call your husband," Clive said. "He must be worried."

"Oh, no. I shouldn't."

Clive studied her. "Well," he said, "It's almost morning."

She nodded and went silent.

He asked if she was hungry.

She said no.

Warmer now?

Yes.

And then his wife appeared and Clive introduced them and they sat together as if it were quite normal to have Lily sitting at the breakfast table. Joy made eggs and bacon and fried potatoes and toast and coffee, and when she finally sat she said that one of her best friends came from the Brethren. She said that she admired Lily's people. Such peace and good will.

Lily nodded, as if this was the truth.

She discovered that she was hungry, and when she finished her food and Joy offered more potatoes she took some. It was warm in the kitchen now and she was sleepy and when Clive pushed back from the table and said, "Let's get you home. Your husband will be worried," she wanted to protest, but she said nothing.

The light was blue and then the sun was up and the sky grew clear and the light was whiter and the snow was blinding. Clive wanted to drive right onto the yard, but Lily insisted that he drop her off at the driveway. She took her suitcase and jumped down from the cab and thanked him.

"Nothing doing," Gerald said. "You'd do the same for me if I was lost and stranded."

Out in the yard, walking towards her house, she passed Mrs. Gerbrandt, who had just come out of the barn. They said nothing to each other, though she was aware of Mrs. Gerbrandt watching her enter the house with her bag. She went upstairs and unpacked and put the bag away and then she ran a hot bath and when she was clean and warm, she towelled dry and dressed. She went downstairs and she made lunch for Johan who, when he came in from the outside, saw her standing at the counter. He stopped when he saw her and he said her name, which was a surprise, and then he came to her and he put his arms around her and he held her. Then he sat down and ate, and as he ate she stood with her back to the window, facing him. She told him that a young man named Clive had picked her up and he and his wife had fed her breakfast. They had talked.

Johan looked up, surprised, and he spoke. "What did you say?"

She said that she had talked about her good life, and her good husband, and her good family. "You don't have to worry," she said.

She said that at night the moon was full. The fields were white as if a soft sunlight was falling onto them. She said that she had wondered how she might describe with words the light, and the fields, and the moon. She said that a deer was standing in the ditch. Its head went up and then it fled out into the field. The moon was so bright.

"The deer fled," she said.